PUFFI

SPACE

Looming above your home ... starship *Vandervecken*. Aboard, the crazed scientist, Cyrus, is planning to unleash a gruesome experiment upon your world, destroying all life as it is known and leaving only hideous mutations in its wake.

YOU are an assassin, a highly-trained fighting machine, expert in the martial arts of twenty-seven different human and alien species. YOU have been chosen to seek out Cyrus on board the *Vandervecken* and bring his evil plans to an end. But beware! Terrifying creatures await you there – part robots, part mutants – all products of the scientist's earlier experiments.

Two dice, a pencil and an eraser are all you need to embark on this thrilling science-fiction adventure, complete with its elaborate combat system and a score sheet to record your gains and losses.

Many dangers lie ahead and your success is by no means certain. Powerful adversaries are ranged against you and often your only choice is to kill or be killed!

The Fighting Fantasy Gamebooks

Steve Jackson and Ian Livingstone
present

SPACE ASSASSIN

Andrew Chapman

Illustrated by Geoffrey Senior

Puffin Books

Puffin Books, Penguin Books Ltd, Harmondsworth, Middlesex, England
Viking Penguin Inc., 40 West 23rd Street, New York, New York 10010, U.S.A.
Penguin Books Australia Ltd, Ringwood, Victoria, Australia
Penguin Books Canada Ltd, 2801 John Street, Markham, Ontario, Canada L3R 1B4
Penguin Books (N.Z.) Ltd, 182–190 Wairau Road, Auckland 10, New Zealand

First published 1985

Made and printed in Great Britain by
Cox & Wyman Ltd, Reading
Filmset in 11/13pt Linotron Palatino by
Rowland Phototypesetting Ltd
Bury St Edmunds, Suffolk

CONTENTS

INTRODUCTION

In this book you play the part of a futuristic assassin sent to capture a tyrannical despot bent on the destruction of your world. You must find the way through the mazes and hazards of his giant spacecraft, the *Vandervecken*, and eventually comfront and capture him.

Before you can begin, however, you must determine your strengths and weaknesses, and select your weapons and armour. For this you will require two dice and a pencil to record scores on the *Adventure Sheet* on pages 18–19. As it is possible that you will not complete your mission on your first attempt, you may wish to take photocopies of the *Adventure Sheet* for future use.

Your Abilities

Your ability to fight, withstand damage and escape from tricky situations is determined by your SKILL, STAMINA and LUCK. On your *Adventure Sheet* you will see sections where these attributes are to be recorded. They are derived as follows:

Roll one die. Add 6 to the result. Enter this total as your SKILL score.

Roll two dice. Add 12 points to the result. Enter this total as your STAMINA score.

Roll one die. Add 6 to the result. Enter this total as your LUCK score.

Using Luck

On occasion, you will be called upon to *Test your Luck*. When this occurs, roll two dice. If the result is *equal to or less than* your current LUCK score, then you have been *Lucky*. If the result *exceeds* your current LUCK score, then you have been *Unlucky*. Each time you *Test your Luck*, reduce your current LUCK score by 1 point. Thus, the more you use your LUCK, the riskier it becomes.

Armour

Being a high-technology assassin you are equipped with the latest in protective equipment – this being a sensomatic armoured pressure-suit which may absorb damage from blasters, grenades or similar weapons. To determine the strength of your armour, roll one die, add 6 to the result and enter the total under the appropriate section on your *Adventure Sheet*.

Whenever you engage in a gunfire duel with an opponent and receive a hit, roll two dice. If the result is *equal to or less than* your current ARMOUR score, then your opponent's shot has not penetrated your armour and thus does not wound you. If the result *exceeds* your current ARMOUR score, then your opponent's shot penetrates your armour and wounds you (see the weapons list below for the effects of wounding).

Each time you roll two dice to determine if an opponent's shot has penetrated your armour, reduce your ARMOUR score by 1 point. Note the similarity of the above procedure to *Test your Luck*.

Selecting Weapons

Roll one die: this represents how many points you have to spend on weapons and to gain additional ARMOUR points. Consult the lists below for the cost and effect of arms and armour.

WEAPON/ARMOUR	COST
Electric lash	1
Assault blaster	3
Grenade	1 each
Gravity bomb	3
Armour	½ per additional point

Note that you must buy either an electric lash or assault blaster before purchasing anything else. So, for instance, if you roll 3, you may acquire one assault blaster *or* an electric lash, a grenade and 2 additional ARMOUR points. The effects in combat of the different weapons are as follows:

Electric lash – a small hand-gun which projects an electric pulse, inflicting 2 points of damage on your opponent's STAMINA.

Assault blaster – a heavy-duty military weapon which inflicts varying amounts of damage. The amount is determined by rolling one die and deducting the result from your opponent's STAMINA. Thus an assault blaster will cause from 1 to 6 points of damage against a target's STAMINA.

Grenade – an area-effect weapon which will cause varying amounts of damage on *all* your opponents in the blast area. The amount of damage is determined by rolling one die for *each* target and deducting the result from that target's STAMINA. Grenades can be used only when the book specifies that it is possible.

Gravity bomb – a heavy-duty demolition bomb for blasting doors, immovable objects, etc. It consists of a microscopic black hole suspended in a time-stasis field. When the stasis field is switched off at detonation, the black hole sucks in and annihilates *everything* within a ten-foot ràdius. The black hole then evaporates into hyperspace, leaving the blast area completely safe.

Hand-to-hand Combat

Hand-to-hand combat is conducted the same as in other Fighting Fantasy books. If you are already familiar with this system you can skip this part of the rules. Otherwise:

1. Combat is simultaneous. Hand-to-hand fighting is a series of clashes in which one combatant will do damage to the other.
2. Roll two dice. Add your opponent's SKILL score to the roll. The total is your opponent's Attack Strength.
3. Roll two dice again. Add your SKILL score to the roll. The total is your Attack Strength.

4. If your opponent's Attack Strength is higher than yours, the opponent has inflicted damage on you – deduct 2 points from your STAMINA.

5. If your Attack Strength is higher than your opponent's, you have inflicted damage upon your opponent – deduct 2 points from your opponent's STAMINA.

6. If both Attack Strengths are equal, both attacks have missed. Start the next Attack Round from step 2 above.

7. Continue this combat until either your opponent's or your STAMINA is reduced to zero.

Note: if you are fighting more than one opponent, you fight them one at a time.

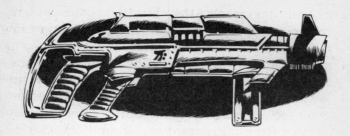

Gunfire

The combat sequences for blasters, grenades and electric lashes are as follows:

1. If you are instructed by the book that it is possible to throw a grenade, you may do so. If so, roll one die for each opponent in the target area and deduct any damage inflicted.
2. After throwing a grenade, if any of your opponents are still alive, you engage them in gunfire or hand-to-hand combat (whichever the book specifies).
3. A gunfire combat round is conducted as follows:
4. Roll two dice. If the result is *greater than or equal to* your SKILL, you have missed. If the result is *less than* your SKILL, you have hit your opponent and inflicted damage on it – deduct as much damage as the weapon you are using causes (see the list under Selecting Weapons, page 12).
5. If your opponent's STAMINA has reached zero, then your opponent has died.

6. If your opponent is still alive, then your fire will be returned: roll two dice. If the result is *greater than or equal to* your opponent's SKILL, your opponent has missed. If the result is *less than* your opponent's SKILL, your opponent has hit you – if the blast penetrates your armour, deduct as much damage as your opponent's weapon causes from your STAMINA. If your opponent's weapon is not specified, then treat it as if it were armed with an assault blaster.
7. Repeat step 6 for each opponent still alive (if you are faced by more than one opponent).
8. If you have not been killed, a new combat round starts from step 4.

Note: if you are faced by more than one opponent you must direct your fire against the first listed until it is killed, then change to the second listed, and so on. Also, if you are involved in a gunfire battle without a weapon, then the amount of damage you inflict on your opponent will be 1 point per hit: you are expert in unarmed combat as well.

Recovering Stamina

If you become involved in any gun battles or other combat you will almost certainly lose some STAMINA points. These may be recovered by taking Pep Pills. Each Pill will restore 5 points to your STAMINA and can be taken at any time. You begin the adventure with 4 Pep Pills – note that there is a section on the *Adventure Sheet* for keeping a record of the number of Pep Pills you have left. Your STAMINA score can never be made to exceed its *Initial* level.

Carrying Equipment

During the course of your adventure you are likely to come across certain items which you may wish to take with you. The maximum number of items (not including weapons) that you can carry at one time is five.

ADVENTURE SHEET

SKILL	STAMINA	LUCK
Initial 10	Initial 21	Initial 11 10
Skill = 9	Stamina = 20	Luck = 8 7
	21 19 20 15 14	7
	18 17	

ITEMS OF EQUIPMENT CARRIED	ARMOUR 12
	Initial Armour =
	12 12

PEP PILLS 4 3

WEAPONS
Blaster
Grenade x2

ENCOUNTER BOXES

Skill= *Stamina=*	*Skill=* *Stamina=*	*Skill=* *Stamina=*
Skill= *Stamina=*	*Skill=* *Stamina=*	*Skill=* *Stamina=*
Skill= *Stamina=*	*Skill=* *Stamina=*	*Skill=* *Stamina=*
Skill= *Stamina=*	*Skill=* *Stamina=*	*Skill=* *Stamina=*

MISSION BRIEFING

For some time, Cyrus, the tyrannical ruling scientist of Od (your local sector), has been harassing your home planet with his warped minions – destructive robots and evil creatures almost certainly of mutant origin. His most usual crime has been to descend upon your planet and kidnap innocent victims upon whom, it is reputed, he practises his malign experiments and surgery. In any event, his victims are never seen again.

Now, however, word has been received that he intends to use your entire world for one gruesome biological experiment in which he will cover the surface of the planet with radioactive isotopes while showering deadly viruses upon all living creatures. The time has obviously come to stop him. To this end, the authorities have appealed to the planetary Assassins' Guild, which has selected you to penetrate into Cyrus's huge starship, the *Vandervecken*, capture him and bring him to justice.

So, armed with the latest and deadliest weapons, trained in twenty-seven different schools of alien and human martial arts, protected by the best in sensomatic armoured pressure-suits, you set off, searching for the *Vandervecken* throughout the local star systems and eventually catching up with it in a relatively isolated system some light years from your home world. It seems to be in the process of refuelling and taking on supplies. You decide that your best bet is to smuggle yourself on board the ship's supply shuttle and let that take you to the *Vandervecken*.

NOW TURN OVER

Secreting yourself aboard the *Vandervecken*'s supply shuttle, you travel from the planet's surface to dock with the main ship. As the shuttle approaches the enormous spacecraft you clamber into an emergency escape airlock and await the sounds of contact. You check your spacesuit and weapons, then rest your hand upon the door release – its hair-trigger mechanism ready to snap down and hurl you into the void. In your headset you can hear the ship's computer counting off the seconds until contact. When it reaches zero you pull the door release and fly out low over the *Vandervecken*'s silver hull, while behind you the shuttle rests like a tiny dart beside the bloated ovoid of its mother ship.

As you skim a few metres over the hull you notice a small iris airlock – your target – ahead of you, protruding slightly like a black disk. Throwing out a magnetic clamp you bring yourself to a halt, floating lazily over the airlock, your shadow cast starkly in front of you. After a few deft movements on the airlock mechanism the iris dilates. You step inside, seal the entrance and fill the airlock with air.

You are in the *Vandervecken*. Stepping out of the airlock, you find yourself at the end of a short corridor which is blocked in front by an impassable security door. Each wall has a small maintenance hatch, across which the legend CAUTION is boldly stencilled. On the steel floor, by the security door, is a small pile of what seems to be organic refuse. If you have a gravity bomb you could use it to blast your way through the security door (turn to **20**); otherwise you could examine the left (turn to **58**) or right (turn to **77**) maintenance hatch, or take a look through the pile of refuse (turn to **39**).

2

You reach another maintenance hatch set at the end of the tunnel.

T MINUS ONE MINUTE

You fling it open. Turn to **120**.

3

Through the hatch is a small room with several large steel conduits rising out of the floor and disappearing into the ceiling. It is from these conduits that the heat you could feel through the hatch emanates. Crossing the room, you come to a sliding door, which you open a fraction and peer through the gap. Before you is a large and (for aliens) fashionably furnished room – odd couches and chairs, tables at just the wrong heights and lights set to just this side of too blue. Seated, reading from electronic resource-sheets, are two rodent-like Fossniks; their white lab coats and tiny pince-nez (for their equally tiny eyes) betray them as being technical types. Will you enter the room and either threaten (turn to **60**) or attack (turn to **41**) these hench-beings of Cyrus, or leave them alone and return to the access tunnel (turn to **172**)?

4

After just one hit the globe goes out of control and spins wildly around the room before disintegrating against one of the walls. Looking around, it becomes apparent that this laboratory is used primarily for biological research: there are the usual instruments of vivisection, electronic monitoring devices and, of course, water-tanks and cages for, respectively, amphibious and terrestrial victims. You find a number of items that may be of some use: a very light can of aerosol labelled NERVE GAS, a packet of three tablets (unlabelled) and a rather huge dead, but fresh, crab. Bearing in mind that you do not wish to become overladen, you may take any two of these items. If you want to try one of the tablets, turn to **42**; otherwise you leave the lab via the door you entered by and proceed through the other door at the 'inspection point'. Turn to **80**.

5

The door slides open and, to your consternation, you find yourself confronted by no less than half a dozen robots of various designs and functions. Several are armed. The room they are standing in is full of tools, hoists and computer-driven workbenches. Several dismantled androids and cyborgs are scattered about in odd places. The robots facing you are quite impassive, but then machines aren't very expressive at the best of times. Will you:

Fight them?	Turn to **43**
Try to talk to them?	Turn to **157**
Assume they are inoperative and enter the room?	Turn to **24**

6

You leave the armoury and inspect the other door in the room where you fought the Pillboxes. Turn to **213**.

7

Roll three dice. If the result *exceeds* your STAMINA, turn to 45. Otherwise you have made it safely across to the western bank – turn to 214. In either case, deduct 1 point from your STAMINA.

8

Having escaped the plant, will you devote some time to having a closer look through this forest (turn to 46) or just attempt to find your way out of it by heading either north (turn to 78), west (turn to 323), south (turn to 179) or east (turn to 84)?

9

The enemy vehicle appears in front of you, exposing its more vulnerable armour. You fire without fear of it retaliating – roll the dice (as previously specified). If you have destroyed your opponent turn to **190** *now*; otherwise the other tank turns around and drives straight at you. Add 1 to your STATUS. Turn back to your previous location to select your move, but ignore the directions to check your STATUS.

10

The door opens into an alcove in the side of a corridor which runs to the left and right. There are no arrows or directions indicating which path should be taken. Will you go left (turn to **200**) or right (turn to **48**)?

11

As soon as you drift over the landing, the anti-gravity force cuts out for a moment, enabling you to scramble away from the centre of the tunnel. You walk down the landing and through the door. As the door shuts, you notice that it seems to melt into the wall and become invisible. Turn to **201**.

12

He glares at you, then faints. You make a cursory examination of the room but, finding nothing, head for the door. Turn to **327**.

13

The Tharn Doppelgänger is vanquished. If you haven't already, you may open the first sleep capsule (turn to **31**); otherwise you leave the room (turn to **126**).

14

After a short walk down a corridor you find yourself in a room occupied solely by seventy or eighty floating black spheres – so black that they look like holes in the air. They drift about the room in a lazy circular motion, touching nothing. On the other side of the room, through the spheres, you can see a door. If you have the Pan-Dimensional Homing Device you can use it, if you want (turn to **128**). Otherwise, will you:

Ignore the spheres and walk straight through the middle of the room to the other door?	Turn to **382**
Try to reach the other side by dodging past the spheres?	Turn to **90**
Go back to the room you just came from and take the left door?	Turn to **381**
Or go back and take the right door?	Turn to **34**

15

'What's the question?' you ask. 'This,' answers the alien. 'What is the next letter in the following sequence: O T T F F S S E?' When you have decided what the next letter in the sequence should be, determine the *number* of that letter (A = 1, B = 2, C = 3, D = 4, etc.), multiply that number by ten (A = 10, B = 20, etc.), and that is the number you should turn to. If the page you turn to doesn't make sense (in context), then you have obviously made a mistake and are destroyed by the creature's disintegrator.

16

If you have either of the items below you could offer one of them to the aliens:

The head of the drink-offering android	Turn to **242**
The aerosol can of nerve gas	Turn to **314**

If you do not possess either of these, then you will have to offer them something else, such as a weapon or a piece of armour (turn to **206**).

17

You offer the jaws to the chief, an act which seems to please both him and his tribe. They perform another short dance and sing what you presume to be their equivalent of 'For He's a Jolly Good Fellow'. Turn to **368**.

18

'Come in, come in,' it urges amiably, waving you forward. 'Tell me,' it continues, 'since you're a person who deals with life and death, consciousness and non-consciousness, do you think that it is possible that one of us is simply the creation of the other's mind? Do you think that you could be dreaming me, or that I could be dreaming you?' What a question! Will you hazard an answer (turn to **132**) or tell the pilot that you really don't know (turn to **170**)?

19

He steps away from you and walks to the other side of the room. Hitting a switch on the wall, he plunges the room into darkness. If you have the infra-red goggles, turn to **298**; otherwise turn to **334**.

20

The gravity bomb blacks out the door for a microsecond with its sphere of annihilation, and creates in soundless destruction a perfectly round hole to the room beyond. Standing on the other side of this newly created entrance is a faceless humanoid robot armed with an assault blaster. It takes in the scene of destruction with seemingly placid detachment, then raises its weapon and takes aim. You will have to fight it.

GUARD ROBOT   SKILL 5   STAMINA 5

If you defeat it, turn to **300**.

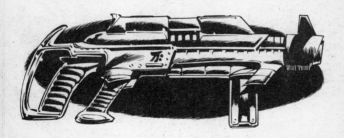

21

You run down the tunnel, dodging pipes and conduits, while the machine's voice follows you:

T MINUS FIVE MINUTES

Turn to **353**.

22

If you have just turned to this location, add 1 to your STATUS. Your vehicle is at point E, facing south. After checking your STATUS below, if you want to move ahead to point H you can turn either to **265** (to finish facing east) or to **193** (to finish facing west); if you want to turn on the spot (E), then turn to **216** to face west, or to **386** to face east. STATUS: if STATUS equals 7, turn to **261**; if it equals 6, 13 or 14, turn to **66**; if it equals 5 or 12, turn to **188**. (Remember to return to **22** though.)

23

Turn to **166**.

24

The robots do not respond in any way to your intrusion into the room. They are obviously not working. Turn to **62**.

25
During your wander among the hills you come upon the granite entrance of what seems to be a large cave. Huge rocks press over it and a narrow path twists into its darkness. Will you enter this cave (turn to 210) or abandon your search and go either north (turn to 64), west (turn to 78), south (turn to 84) or east (turn to 214)?

26
You are on a grass-covered plain which extends to the south, west and east, while to the north it develops into scrubby and broken badlands. Will you go north (turn to 235), west (turn to 159), south (turn to 78) or east (turn to 64)?

27

You are in a choked and stifling forest; huge creepers hang from monstrous trees and the ground is covered in ferns, bushes and other thick undergrowth. You fight your way through it with some difficulty. Roll one die. If the result is even, turn to **65**. If the result is odd, turn to **173**.

28

The enemy vehicle is in front of you, exposing its more vulnerable armour. You fire without fear of it retaliating – roll the dice (as previously specified). If you have destroyed your opponent turn to **190** *now*; otherwise the other tank takes a left turn two blocks ahead and disappears from sight. Add 1 to your STATUS. Turn back to your previous location to select your move, but ignore the directions to check your STATUS.

29

The container is full of ball-bearings. Turn to **181**.

30

The hatch gives way into a small, hot, smelly room, full of pipes and wiring. The most noticeable thing, though, is a tiny, emaciated, quadrupedal alien cowering in the furthest corner from you. Its three eyes roll as if in fear and its innumerable joints knock. It certainly looks terrified of you – but who can tell the ways of aliens? Maybe it's a warning, or a greeting. Will you greet the alien and try to talk with it (turn to **68**), or assume it to be dangerous and either threaten it (turn to **106**) or kill it (turn to **144**)?

31

You start the revive cycle. After a few minutes some sounds of activity arise from within the capsule, which then swings open, letting out a monstrous spider-like creature – a bit bigger in the head (relatively) and smaller in the abdomen than most spiders, but nevertheless a spider. Will you fight it (turn to **69**), run away (turn to **126**), attempt to communicate with it (turn to **107**), or search through your pack for some alternative (turn to **183**)?

32

The security door is featureless and impassable. The only hint of a means of opening it is given by a small hole to the side. Turn to **155**.

33

The enemy vehicle is driving straight at you, aiming to kill with its phaser. It fires – roll one die. If the result is *not* 1, then it has hit you, stripping 1 SHIELD from your defence level. Add 1 to your STATUS. If you have not been destroyed, then you fire back – roll the dice (as previously specified). If you have eliminated your opponent turn to **190** *now*; otherwise turn back to your previous location to select your move, but ignore the directions to check your STATUS.

34

The door leads you down a long and ill-kept corridor; everything is covered in dirt and grime, and quite a few of the lights are missing. A sense of gloom pervades. Eventually the corridor forks; one of the paths has an ageing WARNING sign dangling in front of it, while the other just continues until it disappears into dim reaches. Will you go down the path which has the WARNING sign in front (turn to **378**) or take the other fork (turn to **44**)?

35

When you offer the fruit to the chief he takes a piece, bites it and promptly falls over dead. The rest of the aliens are appalled, and leap at you with needle-sharp spears; the ferocity of the attack breaches your armour. You collapse under the wave of bodies, never to rise. You have failed.

36

Will you engage the Sentinels in a fight (turn to 74) or jump for the hanging girders of the ceiling and, using them as cover, attempt to approach the exit at the other end of the room (turn to 150)?

37

'Oh,' says the disappointed pilot, 'perhaps you're not really such an interesting person after all. Quite boring, actually.' It sighs and turns away. 'I think you should leave now,' it says. Turn to 75.

38

The chute ends in a vast hangar, empty now bar a small starship which is slowly drawing away from its dock. Presently it pulls free of the mother ship and accelerates away into hyperspace. Cyrus has escaped, and you have failed.

39

The pile of refuse, on closer examination, turns out to be the body of a tiny, hunchbacked, alien critter; rags that were once clothes wrap its skin, and its six bony limbs lie tangled beneath it. A trail of blood indicates that it must have crawled out of the right-hand maintenance hatch. Rolling the creature over, you notice that it has an electronic device clasped in one hand; its finger is on the button, and bright wires lead up the arm and disappear into the remnants of a sleeve. Will you remove this device from the body (turn to 141) or leave it alone (turn to 234)?

40

You find yourself in a circular room. In the opposite wall is an airlock door on which is written ESCAPE POD in bold yellow letters. Will you attempt to get through to the pod (turn to 116) or search the room (turn to 154)?

41

You fling the door open and begin firing into the two Fossniks. They are unarmed and unprepared, so you, being a trained assassin, gun them down easily. Looking about the room you discover a security door hidden behind a decorative screen. Will you go through this (turn to 79) or search the aliens' bodies (turn to 117)?

42

The tablet produces a momentary light-headedness followed by a sensation of returning energy. Restore 5 points to your STAMINA. You now have two tablets left, which you may take at any time to restore (per tablet) 5 points to your STAMINA. Leaving the lab via the door you entered by, you proceed through the other security door at the 'inspection point'. Turn to 80.

43

As you are standing in the cover of a doorway you may throw a grenade in, if you have one. If you decide to do this, turn to 81; otherwise turn to 119.

44

The corridor twists into increasing darkness as more and more of the overhead lights fail. It ends at the bottom of a vertical tunnel. Peering up into the dim circular tunnel, you can make out some recessed handholds leading up. Out of the wall by your side a large hoop-shaped lever projects into the corridor – it may be an operating lever for an anti-gravity elevator to take you up the tunnel. Will you pull this lever (turn to 86) or climb up the tunnel using the handholds instead (turn to 360)?

45

You lack the strength to get across, and the fast-flowing current drags you along with it. Presently you hear the sounds of some approaching rapids. Unable to leave the water you are swept down through a series of water-slides, small waterfalls and jumbled rocks. Despite your best efforts you cannot avoid all the hazards: you get wounded by the continual jarring. Roll one die and deduct the result from your STAMINA. Eventually the rapids end and you are swept down the centre of a gigantic chasm. Turn to **324**.

46

You don't find anything other than various exotic forms of vegetation and wildlife. Turn back to **8** and make another choice.

47

The knowledge you have gained from reading the book will allow you to inflict an extra point of damage on the Bivalve every time you hit it. Turn to **85**.

48

The corridor, after a long straight, takes several tight turns and ends at a door. Opening this, you find yourself in an electronics laboratory or workshop; there are small computers, holographic diagnostics and the like set about the room. You don't have time to take much in, though, as a small hovering machine – no bigger than a football, but covered with spinning rotors, sensors and legs – rises out of cover and shoots several electric-blue bolts of energy towards you. You will have to fight it. If the machine hits you, roll one die and subtract the result from your STAMINA.

MICRO-
      HELICOPTER   SKILL 8   STAMINA 2

If you defeat it, turn to **124**.

49

The anti-gravity force cuts out for a moment as you pass over the landing. If you had wanted to stop here you could have, but as you make no move to go down, the force starts up again and carries you off into the darkness. After a short period another landing appears in front of you, this one leading off into a corridor. You realize that it is the place you began from – the tunnel is a ring! Will you alight here and go through the maintenance hatch previously mentioned (turn to **125**) or will you continue with the current and get off at the landing you passed over before (turn to **87**)?

50

After a number of kilometres you see that the path ends in a large aluminium cube also floating, rather paradoxically, in thin air. As you get closer, you see there is a door in the side of the house-sized cube. You cannot see if the path continues out the other end. Will you go through the door (turn to **88**) or turn back and proceed down the left-hand branch of the path (turn to **345**)?

51

The gravity bomb blacks out the door for a microsecond with its sphere of annihilation. When light returns to the scene (having been banished temporarily due to the intense gravitational field around the bomb), you find that the door and part of the wall have vanished. You proceed through the opening. Turn to **14**.

52

The gravity bomb flies into the Toroid's mouth and explodes, or, rather, collapses into a temporary but infinite gravity field, taking the monster with it. Turn to 332.

53

If you have just turned to this location, add 1 to your STATUS. Your vehicle is at point C, facing south. After checking your STATUS below, if you want to move ahead to point F, turn to 136; if you want to turn on the spot to face west, turn to 365. STATUS: if STATUS equals 10 or 11, turn to 188; if it equals 15, turn to 161; if it equals 16, turn to 9; if it equals 1 or 2, turn to 33; if it equals 3, turn to 66. (Remember to return to 53, though.)

54

They run screaming out into the corridor, their chattering gradually diminishing with distance. Looking in the open crate, you see that it is almost full of an orangey-purple fruit. You may try some of this fruit (turn to **388**) or just ignore it, leave the room and proceed down the corridor (turn to **118**).

55

You offer the jaws to the chief, an act which seems to please both him and his tribe. However, when it becomes apparent to them that you want a part of their totem in return, their mood changes to outright hostility. A few of the bigger aliens openly brandish extremely nasty-looking spears. You decide to quit the village before the scene becomes violent. Turn to **361**.

56

'Why, yes,' you say, 'if I could create a whole world in my mind, why not give my creations awareness? But that would mean I would be like a god – an unwitting god, to be sure, but still . . .' you trail off, unsure whether you have overstepped the bounds of decency and sanity.

'Excellent,' says the pilot, 'my very own thoughts! What an amazing brain you have! We must part the best of friends.' He takes you by the arm and points you at a door on which is marked a crescent. 'See that?' he says, 'Through there lies your aim and destiny. Go forth, child of my mind!' Turn to **75**.

57

You cannot find any hidden doors and you do not know where Cyrus is, except that he is probably making good his escape. You have failed.

58

After some difficulty you manage to open the hatch which, due to an oversight on some technician's part, falls off and drags a large mass of high-voltage wiring with it. *Test your Luck*. If you are *Lucky*, turn to **278**. If you are *Unlucky*, turn to **93**.

59

The right-hand tunnel is cluttered but straight, ending after a short distance in a small airtight hatch. Will you open this hatch (turn to **135**) or return to the junction and continue down the left-hand tunnel (turn to **175**)?

60

You take them completely by surprise. They fall to the floor, raise their paws in supplication and beg for mercy. 'We are but humble scientists!' they squeak. 'Have mercy: don't kill us!' You ask them where Cyrus is, but they claim ignorance, saying that they just work in a lab down the corridor (here they indicate a security door behind a decorative screen) and that Cyrus seeks them out when he wants, not they him. You force them to strip, and then tie them up. While they are stripping, you notice that each wears a small, narrow cylinder on a long chain around its neck. When you inquire what these devices are, they inform you that they are electronic keys to open the security doors on board the ship. Using these keys, will you proceed through the security door in this room (turn to **98**) or will you return to the access tunnel (turn to **172**)?

The wall vanishes to reveal a wide corridor occupied by three rather odd creatures arrayed with a variety of domestic cleaning apparatus. The tallest one, having what look like carrots for ears, nose and cranium, is busy cleaning the lights in the corridor with a long hydrovac, while the two shorter creatures, looking like extremely fat bipedal felines with backpacks, are vacuuming the floor. They stop when they see you. 'Looks like an intruder, fellers,' says the tall one. 'Yup, sure does,' answers the others. They advance towards you, threatening with suction tubes. 'Excitement!' cries one. 'Adventure!' yells another. 'Charge!' screams the last. With that, they attack you, vacuum cleaners sucking, hydrovac spewing vapour and steam. You engage them in hand-to-hand combat.

	SKILL	STAMINA
First CLEANER	8	6
Second CLEANER	9	4
Third CLEANER	7	4

If you defeat them, turn to **290**.

62

The room is obviously a facility for repairing and maintaining robots. There are hoists in the ceiling, industrial cutting-lasers and welders by the benches, and other devices for attending to electronic problems. There is nothing of much interest other than the head of an android which you find in a scrap-bucket. This head insists on continually smiling and offering you a wide range of exotic off-world cocktails. You may take this simpering device with you, but its size will cut down the number of additional items you may carry to two. Leaving the room you continue down the long corridor. Turn to 100.

63

The cell is occupied by a battered old man, with scars covering his arms, and bandages and stitches the rest. He starts apprehensively when you open the cell door, but upon seeing the smoking remains of the robot through the narrow entrance he brightens remarkably, telling you of his kidnap and torture by Cyrus and giving you words of encouragement. He doesn't yield much useful information, though, but he knows a little about the pilot of the *Vandervecken*. 'He's a canny machine, that pilot,' the old fellow cackles; 'worries about the strangest things – heh, heh. Mind, if he asks you anythin' 'bout thinkin' or feelin', say you don't know, that's the safest course.' If you haven't already, you can look in the other cell (turn to 318), otherwise you leave the room via the maintenance hatch and tunnel (turn to 134).

64

You are on a grass-covered plain which continues into the east and west. To the north is a forest and to the south are some low, rocky hills. Will you go north (turn to **343**), west (turn to **26**), south (turn to **158**) or east (turn to **102**)?

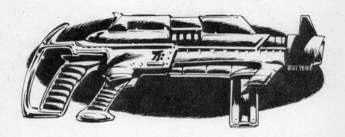

65

A large vine drifts out of a tree behind you and tangles your legs. When you stop to extricate yourself another creeper slides over and wraps itself tightly around your neck. Other vines follow, aiming unerringly for your throat and gripping with vice-like intensity and strength. You are in danger of being choked. Each round that you fight the vines, you will lose 2 points of STAMINA from being choked. You fire at them.

STRANGLING VINES   SKILL 0   STAMINA 12

If you defeat them, turn to **173**.

66

The enemy vehicle is at point-blank range and driving straight at you. It fires. Roll one die: if the result is *not* 1, then it has hit you, stripping 1 SHIELD from your defence level. Add 1 to your STATUS. If you have not been destroyed, then you fire back – roll the dice (as previously specified). If you have eliminated your opponent turn to **190** *now*; otherwise turn back to your previous location to select your move, but ignore the directions to check your STATUS.

67

The case contains an electronic book. It is an encyclopedia of extra-terrestrial life-forms. Turn to **181**.

68

You put your gun aside and make cooing noises. The alien just looks at you, its joints still knocking. You try speaking to it in a friendly manner and, after a while, it seems to calm down a bit. It starts muttering a few words about how it is hurt. So, it can speak! When you ask how it got hurt it shrieks out, 'The nasty, nasty black blobs – they did it!' and here it shows you one of its legs which, you notice, is badly burnt and torn. The alien then resumes its terrified shivering and, no matter how you soothe it, does not speak again. You go back to the tunnel. Turn to **163**.

69

You seem to take the beast by surprise; it looks at you with consternation in its eight eyes while you shoot at it. After hitting it once or twice it scuttles back into its sleep capsule, shutting the door after it. If you haven't already, you can revive the occupant of the second capsule (turn to 274); otherwise you leave the room (turn to 126).

70

You make good time. The path curves for a bit and then ends in a massive grey wall, which seems to extend down towards the alien countryside. Going through the door at the end of the path you find yourself in what is obviously a security nexus. Two dome-headed guards, dressed in black with matching leather straps, boots and holsters, are seated at a wide console, engrossed in a direct telecast from Epsilon-Indi of zero-G fangball which is showing on all ten security monitors in the room. The guards leap to their collective feet when they see you, shine the tops of their scalps and take up assertive postures.

'Who are you?' they ask suspiciously. Will you fight them (turn to 108), attempt to bluff them into thinking you are part of the ship's crew (turn to 146), or look into your pack for some other means of overcoming this obstacle (turn to 184)?

71

To your dismay, all but two of the simulacra spring blasters from their chests, legs, from under their wings and other unlikely places. You will have to fight them *all*! They attack you simultaneously.

	SKILL	STAMINA
First SIMULACRUM	8	3
Second SIMULACRUM	8	3
Third SIMULACRUM	7	3
Fourth SIMULACRUM	6	2
Fifth SIMULACRUM	6	2
Sixth SIMULACRUM	5	2

In the unlikely event that you defeat them, turn to **329**.

72

The tunnel is narrow and circular in cross-section. As you crawl along it you notice, every two metres or so, a ring which appears to be a type of capacitor. The academic interest sparked by this observation is short-lived. You notice that all the air in the tunnel has just been evacuated and that the rings – hundreds stretching to front and rear – have started glowing. Recognition comes instantly – you are in a Mu-Meson projector. The rings flash, sending Mu-Mesons flying down the tunnel, which crash into you and fry you. This is the end of your adventure.

73

If you have just turned to this location, add 1 to your STATUS. Your vehicle is at point G, facing north. After checking your STATUS below, if you want to move ahead to point D, turn to **374**; if you want to turn on the spot to face east, turn to **355**. STATUS: if STATUS equals 7 or 16, turn to **188**; if it equals 9 or 10, turn to **123**; if it equals 8, turn to **66**. (Remember to return to **73**, though.)

74

As you are quite a distance from the robots you may throw a grenade – if you have one. They fire at you simultaneously.

	SKILL	STAMINA
First SENTINEL	8	9
Second SENTINEL	8	9

If you defeat them, turn to **351**.

75

The bridge has three doors leading from it; one is marked with a star, another with a crescent, and the third has the legend COMPUTER stencilled on it. Which will you go through: the star door (turn to **189**), the crescent door (turn to **208**) or the third door (turn to **113**)?

76

As soon as you press the buttons an orange light starts to swim around you. Looking up at Cyrus you can see him laughing hysterically. Something is going wrong: the orange light is concentrating on you and especially on the homing device. Finally it reaches a crescendo of brightness, and the homing device collapses into an impenetrable black hole, sucking you along with it. Pity that you'd never heard that Cyrus was the inventor of a Pan-Dimensional Collapser. You have failed.

77

This hatch opens easily to reveal a long, dark access tunnel crammed with conduits and aluminium lattice-work cutting through the ship. You climb into it and work your way slowly forwards, coming, eventually, to another maintenance hatch through which you can hear a muffled gurgling voice. The tunnel leads on into the darkness. Will you open the hatch (turn to 103) or continue down the tunnel (turn to 134)?

78

You are on a grass-covered plain which rolls on into the north. To the west and south you can see a blue-green forest, while to the east some low, rocky hills rise out of the grass. Will you go north (turn to **26**), west (turn to **121**), east (turn to **158**) or south (turn to **359**)?

79

The door is featureless and impassable. The only clue to a means of opening it is a small hole beside it. Will you search the two aliens for a possible solution to the door (turn to **117**) or will you return to the access tunnel (turn to **172**)?

80

The door opens on to a long, light corridor. Following it, you eventually see another security door on your left. Will you open this (turn to **137**) or continue down the corridor (turn to **398**)?

81

The blast knocks the robots to the floor like skittles. As they do not move or show any activity you enter the room. Turn to **62**.

82

If you have just turned to this location, add 1 to your STATUS. Your vehicle is at point E, facing north. After checking your STATUS below, if you want to move ahead to point B, you can turn either to **167** (to finish facing west) or to **331** (to finish facing east); if you want to turn on the spot (E) then turn to **216** to face west, or to **386** to face east. STATUS: if STATUS equals 4 or 11, turn to **9**; if it equals 5 or 12, turn to **33**; if it equals 6, 13 or 14, turn to **66**. (Remember to return to **82**, though.)

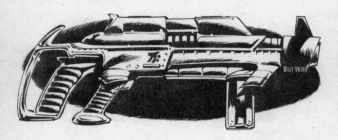

83

You are on a grass-covered plain which continues into the north and west. To the east and south are forests. Will you go north (turn to **341**), west (turn to **250**), south (turn to **27**) or east (turn to **121**)?

84

You are on a grass-covered plain which rolls into the south and east. To the north low, rocky hills rise, and to the west is a forest. Will you go north (turn to **158**), west (turn to **359**), south (turn to **306**) or east (turn to **122**)?

85

You engage it in hand-to-hand combat.

BIVALVE   SKILL 9   STAMINA 8

If you defeat it, turn to **182**.

86

When you pull the lever, the floor drops away from beneath you, plunging you into a garbage-disposal chute from which you are eventually ejected into deep space. You drift away from the *Vandervecken* towards a slow death by suffocation.

87

You drift past the corridor and back into darkness. Presently the other landing appears. Turn to **11**.

88

Opening the door, you discover that the cube is a heavily insulated room containing about a hundred cryogenic sleep capsules – large white sarcophagi in row after row of frost-encrusted silence. Closer examination reveals that only two of these capsules are currently in use. Will you revive one of the occupants of these (turn to 164) or leave the room alone (turn to 126)?

89

'Wrongo, buster,' says the first. 'Tough, Chuck,' says the second. Little panels flick open in their bodies, revealing multiple blasters. You will have to fight them. Turn to 71.

90

You walk slowly forwards. As a sphere approaches, you attempt to dodge to one side. It follows. You jump back but even more of the globes dive at you. For all your gyrating you fail to avoid contact: a sphere touches, bursts and engulfs you in a deadly black flame which sears your suit off and blasts you into oblivion. You have failed.

91

If you have just turned to this location, add 1 to your STATUS. Your vehicle is at point B, facing south. After checking your STATUS below, if you want to move ahead to point E, turn to **22**; if you want to turn on the spot to face west, turn to **167**; if you want to turn on the spot to face east, turn to **331**. STATUS: if STATUS equals 4, 5, 11 or 12, turn to **66**; if it equals 3 or 10, turn to **188**; if it equals 6 or 7, turn to **123**; if it equals 13 or 14, turn to **176**. (Remember to return to **91**, though.)

92

The squirrel-thing sits next to the extra-terrestrial and says, in a clear musical voice: 'See that jerk standing in front of you? He's a tightwad and a dummy – I highly recommend that you blast him.' Not much help there. Will you quickly offer to answer the creature's question (turn to **15**) or attack it instead (turn to **383**)?

93

You are a trifle slow in leaping backwards and thus get lashed by a 77,000-volt cable. Sparks cascade off your pressure-suit as it absorbs the current. Lose 1 ARMOUR point. This hatch is obviously impassable, so you turn your attention to the other maintenance hatch. Turn to **77**.

94

You fire at it, your blaster tearing gaping holes in its beautiful chromium shell. It slumps against the control panel and looks at you with (perhaps) a quizzical expression. 'What a strange person.' It crashes to the floor and bursts into flames. Turn to **75**.

95

You fire at Cyrus's Waldo.

CYRUS   SKILL 9   STAMINA 12

If you defeat him, turn to **400**.

96

The boat handles well and is obviously very tough. You follow the river westwards, hardly having to paddle, except to steer, because of the strong current. Eventually the river describes a wide arc to the south and the sounds of approaching rapids become apparent. The current quickens. If you decide to beach the craft, you can land on either the west bank (turn to **214**) or the east bank (turn to **250**); alternatively, you can shoot the rapids (turn to **287**).

97

You find the central of the three doors to be locked and impassable, whereas the doors to the left and right will open. If you have a gravity bomb, you may be able to blast your way through the central door (turn to **51**); otherwise you can take either the left door (turn to **381**) or the right door (turn to **34**).

98

The door opens on to a long, well-lit corridor. After proceeding down this for a hundred metres or so, you come across a sliding door on the left, while the corridor continues into the distance. Will you open the door (turn to **174**) or keep following the corridor (turn to **229**)?

99

Stepping over to the cage, you unlatch the door and, opening it enough to stick your arm in, reach around for one of the furry critters. As you do this, a number of the little fellows start rushing at the crack in the door. You try to push them back, but before you know it, a whole wave of them have escaped from the cage and are frantically dashing out into the corridor. When you try to catch them, things go from bad to worse, as the rest of them rush out of the cage and run screaming around the room. You forget about getting them back into the cage. Will you concentrate on catching just one of them (turn to **379**) or let them all go (turn to **54**)?

100

The corridor continues onwards, eventually leading you to another door on the left. Will you open the door (turn to **138**) or press on down the corridor (turn to **267**)?

101

You fight the creature in hand-to-hand combat.

SCALLOPIAN FANG   SKILL 9   STAMINA 10

You may run away from the beast at any time for the automatic loss of 2 points of STAMINA. If you choose to run away, turn to **139**. If you defeat it, turn to **196**.

102

You are on a grass-covered plain which rolls on in all directions. Will you go north (turn to **253**), west (turn to **64**), south (turn to **214**) or east (turn to **178**)?

103

The hatch leads into a small lock-up occupied by a faceless humanoid robot armed with an assault blaster and guarding two cells – the gurgling voice you heard is emanating from the first of these. The robot does not seem to have noticed your intrusion. Will you ignore the room and continue up the tunnel (turn to **134**) or attempt to destroy the robot (turn to **228**)? Alternatively, you could attract the robot's attention and try to engage it in a conversation concerning what it is guarding (turn to **192**).

104

You are on a grass-covered plain which continues into the west. To the north and east are forests and in the south some low hills rise. Will you go north (turn to 27), west (turn to 371), south (turn to 289) or east (turn to 115)?

105

The cardboard packet contains a deck of playing-cards. Turn to 181.

106

The alien just shrinks even further into the corner. It says nothing and does nothing, so, seeing little to be gained from this fruitless activity, you go back to the tunnel. Turn to 163.

107

You wave your arms around, roll your eyes and make clicking insect noises – but you soon stop when you remember that spiders often eat insects. The spider, meanwhile, has been watching your antics very closely. 'Very nice,' it says, evidently thinking you were dancing for it. Turn to **145**.

108

As you are standing in the cover of a doorway, you may throw a grenade in at them – however, as they have a console for cover, deduct 1 from the damage result of the blast (thus the grenade will do 0 to 5 points of damage). If the grenade fails to kill them, they will shoot at you simultaneously, whereas you may fire at only one of them at a time.

	SKILL	STAMINA
First SECURITY GUARD	6	4
Second SECURITY GUARD	6	4

If you defeat them, turn to **203**.

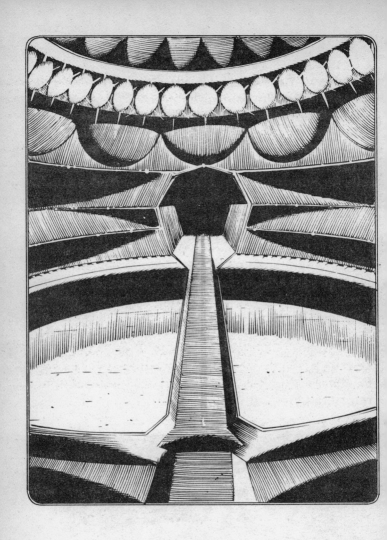

109

The exit leads you down a corridor and into a wide circular room whose floor-space is almost completely taken up by a deep, still pool; the only areas not covered with water are a path leading around the edge of the room and a very narrow bridge without handrails which passes over the middle of the pool. Both of these lead from where you stand to another opening on the other side of the room. Will you cross the room by taking the bridge (turn to 147) or the path (turn to 185)?

110

If you have just turned to this location, add 1 to your STATUS. Your vehicle is at point F, facing north. After checking your STATUS below, if you want to move ahead to point C, turn to 365; if you want to turn on the spot to face west, turn to 391. STATUS: if STATUS equals 3, turn to 176; if it equals 1 or 14, turn to 188; if it equals 2 or 15, turn to 66. (Remember to return to 110, though.)

111

The squirrel-thing sits in front of the extra-terrestrial and begins to speak to it in a clear musical voice: 'Let's get down to business. First I will outline my postulates. One: A is greater than B which is greater than C and so forth. Two: A squared is greater than B squared which is greater than C squared and so forth. Three: the square root of A is . . .' The extra-terrestrial becomes deeply engrossed in the little fellow's rapid and increasingly complex chatter, finally becoming so distracted that you find the opportunity to slip past the two and examine the three doors beyond. Turn to **97**.

112

A blast from the Sentinels smashes through one of the thin aluminium slats you are standing on and hits you. Deduct 2 points from your STAMINA. If this hasn't killed you, you continue to run along the gantry towards the exit. Turn to **207**.

113

The door does indeed lead to a computer. There before you is a large room filled to capacity with still white cabinets, disk drives and air-conditioning. You're rather surprised to find that the *Vandervecken* is controlled by something so primitive. Not even an organic memory! Not even cryogenic cooling!

As you walk through the room you notice another door. Will you go through this door immediately (turn to **208**) or will you wreak a bit of havoc on the ship's computer first by shooting at it (turn to **151**)?

114

You take the cylinder of bearings, open it and roll the contents across the floor towards Cyrus's Waldo, making the device a bit unsteady on its feet. You will have to fight Cyrus, but reduce his SKILL by 1 point. Turn to **95**.

115

You are in an extensive forest of very tall bluish trees, all covered by extremely long thorns. Will you go north (turn to **323**), west (turn to **104**), south (turn to **142**) or east (turn to **179**)?

116

With just a minute to spare, you open the door of the escape pod and slide into the crash couch. You desperately slam the launch button and feel the gratifying sensation of your departure. You have escaped! But your mission to capture Cyrus was a complete failure, and when the *Vandervecken* explodes, the deadly viruses meant for your home planet will be scattered far and wide.

117

You search the bodies but find nothing of any possible use or interest other than that each of the Fossniks carries a small, narrow cylinder on a long chain around its neck. Each of the cylinders has SEC stencilled on it in tiny letters. You take one. If you have already examined the security door, turn to 155; if you want to look at it now, turn to 32. Otherwise you return through the sliding door to the access tunnel (turn to 172).

118

The corridor, after another hundred metres, comes to a dead end. On the wall responsible for sealing the passageway off are two large square buttons side by side. Will you press the left one (turn to 23), the right one (turn to 61), or both together (turn to 156)?

119

You fire at the robots, your blaster punching holes into their inanimate shells. They do not respond or fight back. Realizing that they must be here for repairs, you cease firing and enter the room. Turn to 62.

120

You find yourself in a circular room. In the opposite wall is an airlock door on which is written ESCAPE POD in bold yellow letters. Leaping forward, you attempt to open it. The machine voice counts down: 6 . . . 5 . . . 4 . . . Turn to **154**.

121

You are in a densely packed forest of very tall, thorn-covered trees. The forest stretches as far as you can see in all directions. Will you go north (turn to **159**), west (turn to **83**), south (turn to **323**) or east (turn to **78**)?

122

You are on the west side of a vast, impassable chasm which runs to the north and south. In the bottom of this chasm is a river. The plain you are on extends into the north, south and west; to the east you can see the other side of the chasm. Will you go north (turn to **214**), south (turn to **252**) or west (turn to **84**)?

123

The enemy vehicle is in front of you, exposing its more vulnerable armour. You fire without fear of it retaliating – roll the dice (as previously specified). If you have destroyed your opponent turn to **190** *now*; otherwise the other tank takes a right turn two blocks ahead and disappears from sight. Add 1 to your STATUS. Turn back to your previous location to select your move, but ignore the directions to check your STATUS.

The Microhelicopter crashes to the floor and explodes into flames. The blaze quickly spreads to a nearby computer and then a bank of instruments – it looks as though the whole room could soon be a raging furnace. You will not have long to search it. You race about, examining various items as the heat becomes more and more intense. Eventually, fearing irreparable damage to your spacesuit, you are forced to leave via the door you entered by. However, just before leaving you manage to snatch up *two* of the items that you had been examining. Choose two items from this list:

A plastic cylinder that seems to be full of bearings.

A light plastic case about the size of a pocket calculator.

An unopened cardboard packet with an emblazoned red heart.

A small bottle of black liquid.

Having written down the two items you have chosen, turn to **162**.

125

Behind the hatch is a dark and cramped access tunnel winding into the bowels of the *Vandervecken*. You crawl into and along it, twisting, clambering and losing all sense of direction in the gloom. Presently, you come across another maintenance hatch in the side of the tunnel. Will you open this (turn to 30) or continue down the tunnel (turn to 163)?

126

The only exit from the room is through the door you entered by. Going through this, you trudge the kilometres back along the airborne path, past the T-junction and down the other, left-hand route. Turn to 345.

127

You are on a grass-covered plain which rolls on in all directions. Will you go north (turn to 197), west (turn to 233), south (turn to 250) or east (turn to 341)?

128

An orange glow pervades the room, reflecting off everything except the spheres which remain implacably black. Little doors materialize in front of each sphere and swallow them as they drift over their thresholds; within seconds the entire room is bereft of the globes. The doors evaporate, leaving you easy access to the other side of the room. Before you can stroll across, however, the room vanishes and you find yourself floating in a starry void, light years from anywhere. A stone tablet drifts slowly into view. It is engraved: 'We eliminated seventy-seven spheres of annihilation on your account. As you do not have the means of paying your bill for this service we have taken the liberty of foreclosing and transporting you to this place. Sorry.'

The tablet drifts away, leaving you to spin in the void. You have failed.

129

The tunnel is short, ending in another, but wider, tunnel. You clamber down into this and walk along a bit, becoming aware shortly of a dull vibration in the floor. You stoop to the ground to feel with your gloved hand. At this moment a high-speed intra-vessel transit shuttle tears around a corner in the tunnel and ploughs straight into you at over three hundred kilometres per hour, killing you instantly.

130

If you have just turned to this location, add 1 to your STATUS. Your vehicle is at point D, facing south. After checking your STATUS below, if you want to move ahead to point G, turn to **355**; if you want to turn on the spot to face east, turn to **380**. STATUS: if STATUS equals 8, turn to **33**; if it equals 9, turn to **66**. (Remember to return to **130**, though.)

131

The door opens into a long room occupied by two robot Sentinels flanking the exit at the far end. As you enter, they open fire with a blaze of darting lasers. You duck back into the cover of the doorway and contemplate how to get past them. The two Sentinels are heavily armoured saucer-shaped devices which float about a third of a metre above the floor and which will almost certainly put up very stiff resistance. Glancing back into the room for a moment, you notice that the ceiling is quite low and constructed in an open criss-cross gantry design which runs the entire length of the room. If you have read the book on robotics, turn to **169**; otherwise turn to **36**.

132

'I suppose it might be possible,' you reply, hesitantly. 'Well then,' says the robot, excited, 'obviously you think that you are conscious, so we'll take that as being axiomatic. Given this, do you think that even though I'm a creation of your own mind I might be able to have conscious experiences without your conscious knowledge of such events? Could I be a sort of sub-self of you?' Will you tell the robot that you haven't the foggiest idea of what it's talking about (turn to **37**) or run the risk of seriously offending it by making a very possibly irrelevant answer (turn to **56**)?

133

You find a secret panel by twisting one of the paintings that Cyrus has hanging on the walls. It pops open, revealing a chute. You dive in and slide down in darkness. Did you befriend the robot on the ship's bridge or shoot at the ship's ageing computer? If so, turn to **171**; otherwise turn to **38**.

134

A few metres down the tunnel you find another small hatch. Listening, you can hear nothing – the hatch just feels rather warm. You may continue along the access tunnel (turn to **172**) or open the hatch (turn to **3**).

135

The hatch gives way easily, opening into an octagonal room full of electronic circuitry in large banks running from floor to ceiling. There is little room left among all this paraphernalia for you to squeeze in, but somehow you manage. The room is a dead end with no secrets to give away. Your only discovery is some graffiti next to the hatch: *I hate Cyrus*. Perhaps there is some dissatisfaction among the crew? Pondering this, you leave the room and head back to the junction and down the left-hand passage. Turn to **175**.

136

If you have just turned to this location, add 1 to your STATUS. Your vehicle is at point F, facing south. After checking your STATUS below, if you want to move ahead to point I, turn to **277**; if you want to turn on the spot to face west, turn to **391**. STATUS: if STATUS equals 14, turn to **188**; if it equals 16, turn to **9**; if it equals 1, turn to **33**; if it equals 2 or 15, turn to **66**. (Remember to return to **136**, though.)

137

The door opens to reveal a comfortable-looking room, whose walls are completely lined with ancient bound books, microfilms, electronic resource-sheets and journals. On a table in the centre of the room you find three microfilm volumes that have been left out, presumably for someone to read. One is on the nervous systems of molluscs, the second is about neurotoxins and the third is an article on robotics. They are all possibly relevant, but you only have time to peruse one of them. Which will it be? Write down on your *Adventure Sheet* which volume you choose to read. Having completed this you return to the corridor and proceed along it. Turn to **398**.

138

Through the door is a room with row after row of pressure-suits suspended from bright chromium rails. As you step across the threshold, a black disk the size of a plate cuts from behind one of the rows and flies at you with tremendous speed. You duck at the last moment but the razor-sharp edge of the homicidal device slashes one of your helmet antennae off. It banks sharply and comes back for another pass, aiming directly for your throat. You fire at it.

RAZOR DISK   SKILL 9   STAMINA 1

If you destroy it, turn to **195**.

139

You run from the cave with the beast in hot pursuit. In your efforts to outdistance it, you lose 2 points of STAMINA. Which way will you go now – north (turn to **64**), west (turn to **78**), south (turn to **84**) or east (turn to **214**)?

140

The answer is, of course, the letter N. 'Correct,' says the extra-terrestrial. 'You may pass.' Which door will you go through: the right (turn to **34**), centre (turn to **14**) or left (turn to **381**)?

141

The device is a small black square with a large red button set into it; the wires leading from it attach to a portable power source. Nothing happens when you press the button and, as you can see several other places where some other widget is meant to plug in, you deduce that the device is incomplete. You put it in your pack. Leaving the alien, will you examine the left maintenance hatch (turn to 58) or the right maintenance hatch (turn to 77)?

142

You are on a grass-covered plain which continues to the south, but to the east develops into a broken, scrubby wasteland. To the north is a forest and in the west some low hills rise. Roll one die. If the result is even, turn to 180. If the result is odd, turn to 199.

143

The bottle simply contains ink. Turn to 181.

144

You take careful aim and pull the trigger. The pathetic little alien whimpers and dies. You go over and search the broken little body, but it has no possessions. The realization that you have probably murdered an innocent creature fills you with such disgust that you lose 1 point of SKILL. You go back to the tunnel. Turn to 163.

145

You strike up a conversation, but the spider really doesn't know very much useful information – mainly stuff about insects and trees from its home planet of Ti. It tells a sad tale of being captured by Cyrus for perverse experimentation and, in gratitude to you for having effected its release, it gives you a small sachet of what it calls 'Anti-Mollusc Formula Four' – evidently very popular on the planet Ti. If you haven't already, you may revive the occupant of the second capsule (turn to 274); otherwise you leave the room (turn to 126).

146

They do not look very impressed and, being security guards, they are naturally suspicious. They aim their blasters and tell you to throw down your weapons. Will you do as they say (turn to 239) or will you fight them (turn to 108)?

147

You cross the bridge easily, the lack of a handrail being only mildly disconcerting. You go through the other exit. Turn to 373.

148

If you have the matching piece of this device you may turn to **296**. Alternatively you can attempt to trade something of your own for the device (turn to **224**) or just steal it and threaten the natives with your superior weapons if they kick up a fuss (turn to **251**).

149

The creature cogitates deeply, looking more disturbed and dumbfounded with every second. Its eyes glaze over, it sways slightly and then begins to drool. This deeply distracted state allows you to sneak past it to examine the three doors behind. Turn to **97**.

150

You jump at the ceiling, grab a low girder and swing up on to a narrow walkway, while laser blasts skitter around you. Crouching low, you run along the gantry, ducking constantly as the fire from below smashes with great sparks and splashes of molten metal into the surrounding girder-work. *Test your Luck.* If you are *Lucky*, turn to **207**. If you are *Unlucky*, turn to **112**.

151

You fire into some of the still white cabinets, making them burst into flames and shower you with sparks. A gigantic, evil shudder runs through the entire spacecraft – something essential failing, no doubt. As you want to be able to get off the *Vandervecken* alive, you think twice about destroying more of the computer. You go through the other door. Turn to **208**.

152

If you have either of the items below, you may use one:

Cylinder of bearings   Turn to **114**
Pan-Dimensional Homing Device   Turn to **76**

If you have neither of these (or you choose not to use them), turn to **95**.

153

Will you go north (turn to **359**), west (turn to **115**), south (turn to **235**) or east – either along the northern side of the chasm (turn to **306**) or the southern side (turn to **227**)?

154

Unfortunately you have wasted just a bit too much time. As sirens scream, the machine voice finishes the count-down. The *Vandervecken* is destroyed in a mighty blast and, as a consequence, you are killed.

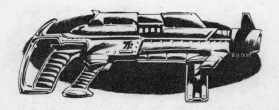

155

'Aha!' you cry. 'The cylinder from the Fossnik is a key for the door.' You push the cylinder into the hole next to the door then watch as the door slides into the roof with a *whoosh*. Turn to **98**.

156

Turn to **166**.

157

Your attempts to engage the machines in any sort of conversation fail. So you tentatively step into the room; the robots continue to ignore you. As you get a closer look at them you notice that they are all in need of repairs. Turn to **62**.

158

You are in the midst of low, rocky hills stretching for kilometres on all sides. Will you have a closer look around the hills' environs (turn to **25**), or just try to get out of them by heading either north (turn to **64**), west (turn to **78**), south (turn to **84**) or east (turn to **214**)?

159

You are on a grass-covered plain which extends to the north, east and west. To the south is a forest. As you trek across this plain you see a shadow gliding over the grass towards you. Looking up you see a massive winged scorpion diving at you with its sting lowered. There is nowhere to run or hide; you will have to fight it hand to hand.

WINGED SCORPION   SKILL 8   STAMINA 6

If you defeat it, turn to **397**.

160

You are on the east side of a vast impassable chasm which runs to the north and south. In the bottom of the chasm is a river. To the north and south you can see flat plains, while behind you, to the east, is a forest. To the west you can see the other side of the chasm. Will you go north (turn to **250**), south (turn to **288**) or east (turn to **27**)?

161

The enemy vehicle appears in front of you, exposing its more vulnerable armour. You fire without fear of it retaliating – roll the dice (as previously specified). If you have destroyed your opponent turn to **190** *now*; otherwise the other tank drives away from you, but remains in sight two blocks ahead. Add 1 to your STATUS. Turn back to your previous location to select your move, but ignore the directions to check your STATUS.

162

To find out what your items are, turn to the appropriate page:

The plastic cylinder	Turn to **29**
The light plastic case	Turn to **67**
The cardboard packet with emblazoned red heart	Turn to **105**
The small bottle of black liquid	Turn to **143**

163

The tunnel continues for a very long time before coming to a dead end. There, at your feet in the floor, is another hatch which you open and drop through. Turn to **201**.

164

The capsules are indistinguishable apart from the life-signs monitors which indicate that the second capsule's occupant has a slightly higher metabolic rate than the first capsule's. Which will you attempt to revive – the first (turn to **31**) or the second (turn to **274**)?

165

You fire! If you have not killed the Toroid after three combat rounds, turn to **384**.

TOROID   SKILL 0   STAMINA 12

If you defeat it, turn to **332**.

166

Without warning, the floor slides away and sends you plummeting down a narrow chute. The floor, now above, moves back into place, plunging you into darkness. The slide continues for a few minutes until the darkness gives way and you find yourself apparently ejected over an alien planet. Strange, though; it looks *very* close and rather doughnut-shaped – not a planetary formation you had been aware could exist. You plummet down towards it, absorbing breathtaking views of wide alien vistas, panoramas and rolling purple hills. Just before you hit the ground at something like 260 kilometres per hour, you mysteriously decelerate to land lightly. You no longer seem to be in the starship but on another planet. (From now on compass points will be used for directional reference.) Turn to **78**.

167

If you have just turned to this location, add 1 to your STATUS. Your vehicle is at point B, facing west. After checking your STATUS below, if you want to move ahead to point A, turn to **349**; if you want to turn on the spot to face south, turn to **91**. STATUS: if STATUS equals 3, turn to **188**; if it equals 10, turn to **33**; if it equals 4, 5, 11 or 12, turn to **66**. (Remember to return to **167**, though.)

168

Which way will you go: north (turn to **289**), west (turn to **102**), south (turn to **83**) or east (turn to **159**)?

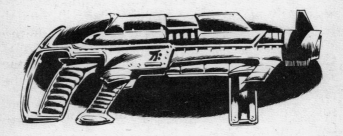

169

The book that you read earlier actually mentioned this type of robot; the knowledge you have thus gained will allow you to inflict 1 extra point of damage every time you hit one of the devices (if you choose to fight them). Turn to **36**.

170

'Oh,' says the pilot, a little hurt at your reply. 'But,' it continues, 'if it were possible, and we assume, just for the argument's sake, that *you* are actually the conscious entity creating this world around you out of your own mind, do you think that I – a creation of yours – might be able to have conscious experiences without your conscious knowledge of such events? Could I be a sort of sub-self of you?' Will you tell the robot that you don't know (turn to **37**) or ignore the rather bizarre questioning and change the subject to something more useful, such as the whereabouts of Cyrus (turn to **389**)?

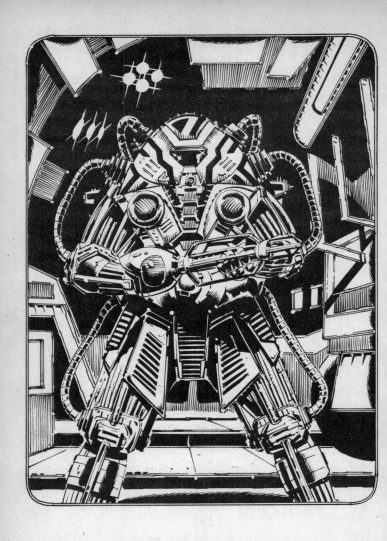

171

When you reach the end of the chute you find yourself in a large hangar housing a small starship. Cyrus, anticipating your pursuit, has climbed into a stevedore Waldo – an enormously powerful machine of roughly human proportions with regard to number of arms and legs but mechanically magnifying the operator's movements to a terrifying degree. Cyrus, using the Waldo, has picked up an industrial laser with which to attack you. Will you fight him (turn to 95) or look in your pack for another means of defeating him (turn to 152)?

172

The tunnel twists and turns through the ship's interior for a considerable distance. Eventually you arrive at a junction, with similar passages disappearing into the darkness to the left and right. To the front, the tunnel ends in a small doorway which is marked:

WARNING
EXTREME DANGER
ENTER ONLY WITH AUTHORITY

You may go left (turn to 175), right (turn to 59) or through the door (turn to 191).

173

Will you go north (turn to 83), west (turn to 160), south (turn to 104) or east (turn to 323)?

174

Through the door is a small kitchen and dining-area; once again everything is decorated in an alien style designed to make human behaviour difficult. The food that is available on the meal-o-matics is, without exception, unpalatable and raw. You do, however, find a couple of high-energy bars which you may take with you (they count as a single item for pack purposes). When you decide to eat these, 5 points will be restored to your STAMINA. Leaving the kitchen, you return to the corridor and proceed along it. Turn to **229**.

175

The left-hand passage is long, wide and straight – a veritable highway in comparison to the tunnels you have traversed so far. It eventually ends in a couple of small hatches; one hatch blocks the tunnel, while the other is set into the wall on one side. Which will you open, the hatch in front (turn to **194**) or the hatch to the side (turn to **266**)?

176

The enemy vehicle appears in front of you, exposing its more vulnerable armour. You fire without fear of it retaliating – roll the dice (as previously specified). If you have destroyed your opponent turn to **190** *now*; otherwise the other tank takes a left turn one block ahead and disappears from sight. Add 1 to your STATUS. Turn back to your previous location to select your move, but ignore the directions to check your STATUS.

177

If you have any of the following you may choose one and employ it against the beast:

Aerosol can of nerve gas	Turn to **232**
Book of extra-terrestrials	Turn to **268**
Pan-Dimensional Homing Device	Turn to **304**

If you have none of these, turn to **340**.

178

After a short distance, you come upon a fast-flowing river which cuts across your path. Will you attempt to swim east across it (turn to **269**), or go north (turn to **253**), west (turn to **64**) or south (turn to **214**)?

179

You are on a grass-covered plain with a large chasm running into it from the east, like a huge axe-cut extending as far as the eye can see. To the north and west are forests. To the south, the plain you are on seems to turn into broken, scrubby country. Will you search for some way down into the chasm (turn to **198**) or go in some other direction (turn to **153**)?

180

The ground collapses, sending you into a deep pit lined with punji stakes. Lose 1 ARMOUR point. After extricating yourself from the stakes you manage to climb out. Turn to **199**.

181

If you have not found out what your second item is, turn back to **162**; otherwise you go back down the corridor and then along the left-hand path – turn to **200**.

182

You dive down to the submarine and climb through the airlock. Safe! There is only one control for the submarine: an on/off switch set into the arm of a chair in the conning tower. You turn this to *on*. The submarine moves, gliding into a tunnel in the lake bed. The journey takes a while and allows you some much needed rest – restore 4 points to your STAMINA. Eventually you surface into a large room, half of which is a pool of water for the submarine, while the other half looks strangely like the interior of the *Vandervecken*. Climbing from the conning tower into the dry half of the room, you see that there is only one exit. You go through it. Turn to **309**.

183

If you have either of these items, turn to the appropriate page:

Large fresh crab	Turn to **202**
Electronic book of extra-terrestrials	Turn to **238**

If you have neither of these, then you must either fight it (turn to **69**), run away (turn to **126**) or attempt to communicate with it (turn to **107**).

184

If you have any of the items below, choose which one you will use and turn to the appropriate page:

Aerosol can of nerve gas	Turn to **275**
Deck of cards	Turn to **311**
Container of ball-bearings	Turn to **347**
Pan-Dimensional Homing Device	Turn to **396**

If you have none of these you will either have to fight them (turn to **108**) or bluff them into letting you through (turn to **146**).

185

When you are about halfway around the pool a series of ripples spreads across the face of the water. You hurry along but notice, to your horror, that tentacles are rising out of the pool's edge and crawling, like slimy green serpents, towards you. Before you can run, you are surrounded. Out of the water rise bloated green bodies, ghastly yellow eyes glinting and hungry beaks clicking. Confronting you are two creatures which resemble both man and octopus. Will you fight them (turn to 204) or search through your pack for some other means of defence (turn to 240)?

186

You give it a piece of fruit. The squirrel-thing bites into it heartily and produces a low, satisfied purr. After eating, it climbs on to your shoulder and, holding on tight, falls asleep. You pocket a couple more pieces of this fruit for later use, then leave the room and head up the corridor. Turn to 118.

187

The two pieces plug together to form a black oblong with two red buttons. Once the two pieces are together they begin to hum and one edge lights up with the legend:

**PAN-DIMENSIONAL HOMING DEVICE –
EMERGENCIES ONLY**

Count it as one item for pack purposes. Turn to 368.

188

A blast from the enemy vehicle's phaser smashes into your tank, stripping 1 SHIELD from your defence level. You can't be sure which direction the fire came from because you can't see to the rear or side, only forwards (and there's nothing in sight there). Add 1 to your STATUS. Turn back to your previous location to select your move, but ignore the directions to check your STATUS.

189

The door leads you to a long corridor which ends in a blank wall. When you touch the wall, to see if there are any hidden doors, all the lights go out and are replaced by an other-worldly blue haze. A high-pitched whine starts up at the other end of the corridor, and small electric flashes arc down towards your end. You realize, too late, that you are in a particle accelerator. A bright cloud of positrons, accelerating to near light-speed, flies down the corridor and crashes into you – removing you from this world in a puff of photons.

190

The lights in your tank go out and you feel your chair rising. Hatches open overhead and then shut below you, as you pass upwards. Suddenly, you are in free fall, in a weightless environment, the chair left behind. You roll over and over, all sense of direction lost. A pinprick of light becomes apparent, growing by the second until, with a rush, it is around and past you. The journey has taken you into a long, light, zero-gravity transit tunnel – generally pretty fast and safe travel, but in your case, as the tunnel up ahead is occupied by a man-eating Toroid, just fast – all too fast. The Toroid looks pretty much like an enormous eyeless dough-nut with innumerable fangs set in its inner circle – an inner circle (or mouth) that you are flying to-wards at great speed. If you have a gravity bomb you could send this down before you into the beast's maw (turn to 52); otherwise you will have to shoot at it (turn to 165).

191

The hatch gives way easily, and a slight sigh of air indicates a small difference in pressure between the tunnel and what lies beyond. Perhaps no one has been this way for quite some time. On the other side is a long narrow room – almost a tunnel – garishly lit by red fluorescent tubes running along all its ver-tices. In the middle of the opposite wall, in the centre of a pulsating neon cross, is a box. Will you investigate the box (turn to 342), or leave the room and go either right (turn to 59) or left (turn to 175)?

192

'I say . . .' you say, to attract its attention. Before you can finish however, the robot spins, aims and fires – the blast smashes into the tunnel behind you and showers the area with molten metal. You will have to fight it. Turn to **228**.

193

If you have just turned to this location, add 1 to your STATUS. Your vehicle is at point H, facing west. After checking your STATUS below, if you want to move ahead to point G, turn to **73**; if you want to turn on the spot to face north, turn to **313**. STATUS: if STATUS equals 5, 6, 12, 13 or 16, turn to **188**; if it equals 8, turn to **261**; if it equals 7, turn to **66**. (Remember to return to **193**, though.)

194

The hatch gives way into a circular airlock with two doorways – one is labelled ESCAPE POD and the other is a security door. If you have picked up a cylindrical security key from an earlier encounter you may proceed through the security door (turn to **356**); otherwise you will have to go back to the tunnel and go through the other hatch (turn to **266**).

195

One good hit smashes the disk into tiny fragments, which bounce harmlessly off your armour. You inspect the room. The pressure-suits are not terribly useful to you, as you already have one, but at the end of one rack you find something that you immediately recognize as being battle armour, constructed of a light fibrous polymer that is extremely resistant to all forms of attack. If you wish to wear it, turn to 231; otherwise you lay it aside, leave via the door you entered by and continue up the corridor (turn to 267).

196

The beast is vanquished and you are master of its cave. Looking around, you find very little – only bones and, in one niche, an enormous pair of carnivore jaws which you may take if you wish. Resting in the safety of the cave you recover 5 points of STAMINA. Eventually, though, you must leave. Which way will you go: north (turn to 64), west (turn to 78), south (turn to 84) or east (turn to 214)?

197

After a short distance you come upon a fast-flowing river which cuts across your path. Will you attempt to head north by swimming across this turgid water (turn to 305), or go east (turn to 341), south (turn to 250) or west (turn to 233)?

198

You find some very rough-cut and dangerous-looking stairs hacked into the side of a cliff, which wind down into the chasm. Will you go down these stairs (turn to **270**) or in some other direction (turn to **153**).

199

Will you go north (turn to **115**), west (turn to **289**), south (turn to **159**) or east (turn to **235**)?

200

The corridor leads past a door on your right. Will you continue down the corridor (turn to **308**) or go through the door (turn to **236**)?

201

You are in a very large room with a rather peculiar floor-space – half of it is taken up by a pool of water running the entire length of the room. At the other end of the dry space, which also runs the length of the room, you can see a door. Will you investigate the pool (turn to **237**) or the door (turn to **309**)?

202

You take the crab out and throw it at the spider's feet. It looks at it, tentatively turns it over with a claw and says, 'Why, thanks.' It eats the crab with some enthusiasm. Turn to **145**.

203

The guards are vanquished, but a red light is flashing on the video controls – perhaps somebody or something has been alerted. You had better hurry. The room has two other exits; one is a security door and the other is a simple manual sliding door. If you don't already have one, you may take an assault blaster from one of the guards. Which door will you go through – the security door (turn to **109**) or the sliding door (turn to **257**)?

204

If you have a grenade you may throw one into the pool. If you decide to throw a grenade, turn to **276**; otherwise turn to **312**.

205

The second button depresses safely. When you press the third, the dial pops free of the floor, revealing the contents of the safe – well, not really a safe, but a booby-trap, for there, sunk into the floor, is a gravity bomb which would have been set off had you pressed the wrong sequence of buttons. It is now safe to handle, though, so you may add it to your weapon list. Which exit from the room will you take: the door in front (turn to **80**) or the door to the side (turn to **319**)?

206

You offer the item to the chief, an act which seems to please both him and his tribe. However, when it becomes apparent to them that you want part of their totem in return, their mood changes quite rapidly to outright hostility. A few of the bigger aliens openly brandish extremely nasty-looking spears. You decide to quit the village before the scene becomes violent. Turn to **361**.

207

You reach the end of the gantry on the other side of the room. Almost directly below are the Sentinels, busily blasting away the ceiling around you. Between them, only a couple of metres away, is the open exit. Will you:

Attempt to swing down from the ceiling, between the Sentinels and straight through the exit?	Turn to **243**
Engage the Sentinels in a fight?	Turn to **279**
Jump on to one of the Sentinels to send it out of control while shooting at the other?	Turn to **315**

208

The door opens into a spacious room. There are deep chairs, paintings, off-world rugs, book-shelves lined with vellum-covered volumes and there, in one of the chairs, is Cyrus! He looks at you in a rather startled way. With nervous haste he puts down the book he was reading and starts to his feet. 'Er . . . welcome,' he begins. 'Can I offer you a drink?' Will you accept his offer and chat with him awhile before making the arrest (turn to 244) or will you move straight in for the kill and capture him immediately (turn to 280)?

209

As you pull the lever down, all the red lights in the room begin a long, slow pulsing. A very low, menacing tone sounds in time with the lights. You wait breathless for a few minutes but nothing else seems to happen. The lights and tone continue to pulse. You can either pull the other lever (turn to 245) or leave the room (turn to 335).

210

Inside the cave you are confronted by a massive furry many-legged beast with huge teeth, bulging eyes and razor talons. It roars and rushes forward when it sees you. It looks so ferocious that you fumble and drop your blaster. Will you fight it (turn to 101), run away (turn to 139) or use one of your pack items (turn to 177)?

211

In the fight, the robot will fire twice per combat round, each hit doing 2 points of damage to your STAMINA.

GUARD ROBOT   SKILL 7   STAMINA 6

If you defeat it, turn to **247**.

212

Your carefully aimed shot kills the man instantly, and sends his body sprawling on the floor. Turn to **248**.

213

This door has two short black levers protruding from it, but is otherwise indistinguishable from any other door on the *Vandervecken*. The door fails to open when you use the electronic cylinder key, so you resort to pulling the levers. Will you pull the left lever (turn to **10**), the right lever (turn to **23**) or both (turn to **156**)?

214

You are on a grass-covered plain which rolls to the south, east and north. In the west some low, rocky hills can be seen. Will you go north (turn to **102**), east (turn to **286**), south (turn to **122**) or west (turn to **158**)?

215

The structure, as you approach it, turns out to be a short pier extending out into a rapidly flowing river. Moored to the pier are several sturdy-looking canoes. You may take a canoe and paddle down the river westwards (turn to **96**), or ignore them and walk north (turn to **289**), west (turn to **102**), south (turn to **83**) or east (turn to **159**).

216

If you have just turned to this location, add 1 to your STATUS. Your vehicle is at point E, facing west. After checking your STATUS below, if you want to move ahead to point D, you can either turn to **374** (to finish facing north) or to **130** (to finish facing south); if you want to turn on the spot (E) then turn to **82** to face north, or to **22** to face south. STATUS: if STATUS equals 5 or 12, turn to **188**; if it equals 9, turn to **261**; if it equals 6, 13 or 14, turn to **66**. (Remember to return to **216**, though.)

217

The forest is just what it seems to be, a forest. You abandon your search and go either north (turn to **227**), west (turn to **235**), south (turn to **64**) or east (turn to **253**).

218

You lean over the prone figure and try to prise open its claws from the disintegrator it was holding. As you do this, the Deity explodes violently – roll one die and subtract the result from your STAMINA. If you are still alive, you find that the weapons are now simply useless hunks of debris. You leave the room via the other exit. Turn to **254**.

219

The path runs for quite a few kilometres before ending at a small aluminium cube which, like the path, is hanging in mid-air. As you get closer you see that the path ends at a door in the side of the cube, while beside the door is parked a rapid-transit two-seater commuter. Will you enter the cube (turn to **395**) or jump into the commuter and head back to the T-junction and down the left-hand branch of the path (turn to **70**)?

220

You fight it in hand-to-hand combat.

THARN
 DOPPELGÄNGER   SKILL 8   STAMINA 6

If you defeat it, turn to **13**.

221

'Yeah?' exclaims the first. 'We could be out of a job soon,' says the other. 'Better pack then.' You leave them chatting about their possible futures. Turn to **329**.

222

You take the homing device in hand, but a green tentacle flies from one of the mutants, snatches the device and flings it into the centre of the pool. Not much chance of using it now – cross the device from your Equipment List. You will have to fight the mutants. Turn to **204**.

223

If you have just turned to this location, add 1 to your STATUS. Your vehicle is at point A, facing east. After checking your STATUS below, if you want to move ahead to point B, turn to **331**; if you want to turn on the spot to face south, turn to **349**. STATUS: if STATUS equals 3 or 4, turn to **33**; if it equals 10, turn to **66**; if it equals 5, 11 or 12, turn to **261**; if it equals 8 or 9, turn to **188**. (Remember, if you have to turn to one of the numbers above because of your STATUS, make a note of where you are – **223** in this case – so you can return here to decide where to move.)

224

What will you use to trade for the part:

A piece of technology?	Turn to **16**
A large set of carnivore jaws?	Turn to **55**
A few pieces of orangey-purple fruit?	Turn to **35**

225

'Check,' says the first. 'Ditto,' says the second. They swivel back on their pedestals and proceed to ignore you. Passing them, you are confronted by the second pair of creatures. They turn and speak: 'Up is up and down is down.' 'But do they really exist or are they ghosts?' adds the second. What will you answer: that they are real (turn to **272**) or not (turn to **387**)?

226

He prattles on about how he loves a good bet, a good card game. He hunts around in the drawer of a desk, presumably for some cards. Presumably. He comes out of the drawer, head up, with a gun which he points at you. 'So, they thought they could get rid of me using just one of their so-called assassins, hey?' he asks derisively, waving the pistol at you as he paces up and down the room. 'A whole planet couldn't dispose of me! They will pay, how they will pay!' He slams a switch on the wall, plunging the room into utter darkness. If you have the infra-red goggles, turn to **298**; otherwise turn to **334**.

227

You are on the south side of a vast impassable chasm which runs from the west to east. The bottom is a flat plain. You are on a narrow strip of grassy plain, which continues to the west and east. To the south is a forest and to the north you can see the other side of the chasm. Will you go west (turn to **179**), south (turn to **343**) or follow the chasm east (turn to **288**)?

228

As you have the hatch for cover you may lob a grenade in at the machine.

GUARD ROBOT   SKILL 7   STAMINA 6

If you defeat it, turn to **264**.

229

The corridor ends in a circular room occupied by a squat, armless, tripedal robot. This robot, which has a pair of electric lashes projecting from its chest, squawks as you approach, 'Halt: inspection point.' Will you attempt to bluff your way past the machine (turn to **301**) or simply attack it (turn to **211**)?

230

Opening the door, you step into a room largely taken up by a glass cage of tiny screaming creatures. They all have six legs and bulging eyes, and most have thick black fur – the odd ones out having been shaved, for no apparent reason. They are all leaping about their cage in great agitation, swinging from overhead bars and rattling at the door. The only other thing in the room is a large open crate some metres from the cage. Will you try to have a closer look at one of the creatures (turn to **99**) or look in the crate instead (turn to **372**)?

231

You swap your old suit of armour for this new one – raise your ARMOUR points to 14. However, as this new suit is bulkier than your own, you will have to decrease your SKILL by 1 point. You leave the room and continue up the corridor. Turn to **267**.

232

You spray the beast in the face and, after a fraction of a second, it rolls over dead. It is a fortunate thing that you still have your spacesuit on. It is unfortunate, however, that you have exhausted the contents of the can – cross it off your Equipment List. Turn to **196**.

233

After a short distance you come upon a fast-flowing river which cuts across your path. Will you attempt to swim west, to the other side (turn to **305**), or go north (turn to **197**), east (turn to **341**) or south (turn to **250**)?

234

The alien doesn't seem to have anything else to offer. Leaving it, will you examine the right maintenance hatch (turn to **77**) or the left maintenance hatch (turn to **58**)?

235

You are on a broken plain covered by rocks, low red shrubs and large black burnt patches. If you have been among these red shrubs before, turn to **307**; otherwise turn to **271**.

236

The door leads you into a small room whose walls are covered with shelves which, for the most part, are filled with electro-memory cassettes. On a table set against the middle of the opposite wall is a machine for copying the contents of these tapes on to others. You walk across to it and find there is a cassette already in the machine, waiting to be copied. If you want to take this item, add it to your Equipment List. You inspect the cassettes on the walls, but find that they all seem to be blank. Disgruntled at not finding anything more useful, you return to the corridor. Turn to **308**.

237

The pool, on closer examination, reveals itself to be a swiftly flowing body of water rushing out from under the wall at one end of the room and disappearing equally rapidly under the wall at the opposite end. Through the distorted surface you can see strange metallic shapes – rails, machines and clamping devices – under the water. Will you ease yourself into the water to identify these devices (turn to **273**) or leave the room via the door on the dry side (turn to **309**)?

238

You take the book out of its cover and point it at the spider. The book tells you that the spider is a Vert from the planet Ti, and that it is intelligent and probably peaceful. Turn to **145**.

239

You put your weapon down at your feet, much to the satisfaction of the guards. They keep their blasters trained on you while they drag your equipment away to the centre of the room. They then decide to kill you, as you are obviously an intruder. What can you do? You dive for your weapons in the middle of the room. *Test your Luck*. If you are *Lucky*, the guards get to shoot at you once each before you fire back. If you are *Unlucky*, the guards get to shoot at you twice each before you return fire. They fire at you simultaneously.

	SKILL	STAMINA
First GUARD	6	4
Second GUARD	6	4

If you defeat them, turn to **203**.

240

If you have any of the items below, choose which one you will use and turn to the appropriate page:

Aerosol can of nerve gas	Turn to **348**
Pan-Dimensional Homing Device	Turn to **222**
Bottle of ink	Turn to **258**
Anti-Mollusc Formula Four	Turn to **394**

If you don't have any of these, you will have to fight them (turn to **204**).

241

If you have just turned to this location, add 1 to your STATUS. Your vehicle is at point I, facing north. After checking your STATUS below, if you want to move ahead to point F, turn to **110**; if you want to turn on the spot to face west, turn to **277**. STATUS: if STATUS equals 2 or 3, turn to **28**; if it equals 15, turn to **33**; if it equals 1 or 16, turn to **66**. (Remember to return to **241**, though.)

242

When you take the head out of your pack it smiles at the chief and says: 'Good day, sir. May I offer you an Antares Red?' It creates a sensation among all present. When it becomes apparent to them that you are actually offering them *this* for the tip of their totem pole, they can't fall over themselves fast enough to make the deal. You get the part. If you have the matching half of this device, turn to **187**; otherwise turn to **368**.

243

Test your Luck. If you are *Lucky*, turn to **297**. If you are *Unlucky*, turn to **333**.

244

He goes to the drinks' cabinet, pours you a large Antares Red, motions you to be seated and then sits next to you. 'So, you have come to take me into custody?' he asks. You nod and take a sip of your drink. You inform him of his crimes against society and how, if he's lucky, he'll only get ninety-nine years instead of the chair. He nods pensively and seems repentant. It is at this moment that you feel decidedly ill. You hold your head as waves of nausea and unconsciousness sweep over you. He's drugged your drink! Roll three dice. If the result is *equal to or greater than* your STAMINA, turn to **316**. If the result is *less than* your STAMINA, turn to **352**.

245

You pull the lever down – the fatal connection is made. The red lights begin to flash with a strobe-like rapidity, a screaming siren starts up and a great rumbling goes through the ship. From all around you a deep machine voice booms out:

REACTOR CORE NOW UNSHIELDED
TERMINAL MALFUNCTION IN T MINUS
TWO MINUTES
DESTRUCTION OF VANDERVECKEN WILL FOLLOW IN
T MINUS SIX MINUTES

Realizing that you've really done it this time, you run from the room, throwing yourself through the hatchway into the tunnel beyond. Will you take the left tunnel (turn to **21**) or the right tunnel (turn to **281**)?

246

When you are within fifty metres of the nearest hut, a loud hubbub starts up as about twenty aliens, looking like fierce little easter eggs with bushes of hair, come streaming out of the village toward you. As the aliens near, a higher-pitched chanting and wailing starts up from an unseen source in the village. Will you stand fast (turn to **336**), open fire on them (turn to **282**) or flee (turn to **361**)?

247

The robot falls over sideways, thick black smoke pouring from its shell. The room has two exits: a security door in front (on the opposite side of the corridor entrance) and another to the side. Will you inspect the remains of the robot (turn to **283**), or go through either the door in front (turn to **80**) or the door to the side (turn to **319**)?

248

You climb through the hatch, look around the room and search the man's body. The room is full of electronic measuring-devices of the sort used in the repair and maintenance of complex electronic systems. None are of any particular use to you. The only item of any interest is a small, narrow cylinder which the man wore around his neck on a long chain. Thinking this might be a key, you approach the security door and put the cylinder in a hole next to it. The door opens. Turn to **356**.

249

The door opens to reveal what is obviously an armoury. There are racks of guns, boxes of ammunition and other interesting devices. If you have not taken a weapon from a robot yet, you may take an assault blaster from one of the racks and add it to your weapon list. You also find two small cases, although, due to their weight, you may take only one. One looks as if it contains explosives, while the other seems to contain a strange pair of goggles. Write down which case you decide to take with you. This lucky find boosts your spirits – restore 4 points to your STAMINA and add 1 LUCK point. You leave via the door you entered by. Turn to **285**.

250

You are on a grass-covered plain which spreads to the south, east and north. To the distant west you can see some hills rising. Will you go north (turn to **127**), east (turn to **83**), south (turn to **160**) or west (turn to **322**)?

251

You push past the chief and his advisers, and make a grab for the totem pole. Instantly, hordes of angry warriors leap at you with previously hidden spears. Most of their thrusts are turned by your armour, but such is the intensity of their attacks that several spears force their way through and make fatal contact. You collapse under the angry wave, never to rise. You have failed.

252

The plain you are on suddenly ends at a precipice. You are on the edge of the intersection of two vast chasms, one coming down from the north, the other from the west, forming a gigantic backward L. Looking down into the bottom, you see a wide lake teeming with life; there are also dark submerged shapes which might be large water animals or perhaps machines. There is no obvious way to get down to find out. Will you follow the chasm north (turn to **122**) or west (turn to **306**)?

253

You are on a grass-covered plain which extends into the north and south. To the west is a forest, while to the east some low hills rise. Will you go north (turn to **288**), west (turn to **343**), south (turn to **102**) or east (turn to **289**)?

254

A solitary corridor twists past the exit for a while before ending at a door. You open this and step through. As the door shuts behind you, you notice that it blends into the wall – looks like there's no way back now. Turn to **201**.

255

You stride boldly across the floor, stepping on your carefully selected tiles and reaching the other side in one piece. You go through the door. Turn to **131**.

256

If you have either of the items below, you may use one of them:

Book of extra-terrestrials   Turn to **364**
Pan-Dimensional Homing Device   Turn to **328**

If you have neither of these, you will fight it (turn to **220**).

257

The door leads to a small kitchenette with a delightful aroma – a pot of coffee is sitting, begging to be drunk, and on a sideboard are some fresh sandwiches! Will you stay here for a while to eat (turn to **293**) or will you go back into the security nexus and through the other exit (turn to **109**)?

258

You open the bottle and throw the ink into the pool where it spreads like a great dark cloud and strikes some primeval genetic chord in the monsters, perhaps of panic. At any rate, they dive into the water and disappear from sight. You run to the exit. Turn to **373**.

259

'What a stupid question,' it says, taking steady aim with its disintegrator. It looks as though you're going to have to fight it. Turn to **383**.

260

If you do not have a spare piece of high-tech equipment to trade, then you will have to give either a weapon – if you have a spare – or 2 ARMOUR points. You offer the item to the chief, an act which seems to please both him and his tribe. Turn to **368**. If you don't have anything to give, then you must leave the village (turn to **361**).

261

The enemy vehicle appears in front of you, exposing its more vulnerable armour. You fire without fear of it retaliating – roll the dice (as previously specified). If you have destroyed your opponent turn to **190** *now*; otherwise the other tank takes a right turn one block ahead and disappears from sight. Add 1 to your STATUS. Turn back to your previous location to select your move, but ignore the directions to check your STATUS.

262

As you lunge over towards him he side-steps and grabs a mechanical device from a coffee-table. 'Stop!' he cries. 'Don't move. This device is a very complicated piece of machinery that I have been working on of late. It fires a guided armour-piercing dart. It never misses. Now, stand aside.' Will you do as he says (turn to **19**) or go for him regardless (turn to **370**)?

263

Turn to **209**.

264

The robot terminates. If you don't already possess one, you may add the machine's assault blaster to your weaponry. You climb into the room, the only sounds now being the crackle of small circuits popping in the robot's chest and the odd stifled cough from the first cell. Which cell will you look in first, the one with sounds emanating from it (turn to **63**) or the silent one (turn to **318**)?

265

If you have just turned to this location, add 1 to your STATUS. Your vehicle is at point H, facing east. After checking your STATUS below, if you want to move ahead to point I, turn to **241**; if you want to turn on the spot to face north, turn to **313**. STATUS: if STATUS equals 5, 6, 12 or 13, turn to **188**; if it equals 1, turn to **176**; if it equals 7, turn to **66**; if it equals 16, turn to **33**. (Remember to return to **265**, though.)

266

Through the hatch is a tiny dark room cluttered with books, small electronic devices, a bunk and other furniture. A man in white overalls, an electronic meter strapped to his waist, is slumped on the bunk with his face buried in his hands. He has not noticed you, nor is he making any noise. A security door in the opposite wall is the only exit from the room. Will you:

Attack him?	Turn to 302
Threaten him to gain some information?	Turn to 320
Talk to him and try to befriend him?	Turn to 284

The corridor leads on for a great distance before making a sharp turn. Following it, you stumble, immediately after the turn, into a circular chamber filled by eight Portabot Pillboxes. These little devices stand about a third of a metre high, are armoured, armed and convenient to carry about in packs of four to defend areas where more cowardly sorts would refuse to venture. As you leap back into the cover of the corridor they pursue you with a withering fire. You will have to fight them. If you have any grenades you may throw a couple into the room; a gravity bomb (if you have one) will ensure a knock-out on all the devices.

	SKILL	STAMINA
First PORTABOT	7	2
Second PORTABOT	7	2
Third PORTABOT	7	2
Fourth PORTABOT	7	2
Fifth PORTABOT	7	2
Sixth PORTABOT	7	2
Seventh PORTABOT	7	2
Eighth PORTABOT	7	2

If you destroy them, turn to 303.

268

You point the book at the charging beast and press a button. 'It's a SCALLOPIAN FANG,' it screams. *'Run!'* Will you run (turn to **139**) or stand and fight (turn to **101**)?

269

Roll three dice. If the result *exceeds* your STAMINA, turn to **45**. If the result is *equal to or less than* your STAMINA, you have made it safely across to the other side – turn to **127**.

270

As you climb down the stairs, rocks slide from under your feet and whole steps disintegrate as you test your weight on them – it is a continual battle to stay upright. Roll three dice. If the result *exceeds* your STAMINA, you slip and tumble down the stairs. If you do slip, roll one die and deduct the result from your STAMINA. Eventually, however, you make it to the bottom of the chasm and head east along the floor, flanked by enormous granite cliffs. After a few kilometres you arrive at the shore of a wide, still lake which has formed across a turn in the chasm. There is no way to walk past it and no point in going back, so, having zero risk of drowning in your spacesuit, you decide to swim across it. Turn to **324**.

271

You accidentally brush against one of the shrubs: it explodes violently, leaving a large burnt patch on the ground and burning your spacesuit – lose 1 ARMOUR point. Turn to 307.

272

'Dear oh dear,' says the first. 'What a dope,' continues the other. Little panels flick open in their bodies, revealing multiple blasters. You will have to fight them. Turn to 71.

273

You climb into the water, lose your grip and get swept under the far wall. For a long time you are carried along, here and there, in total darkness. Eventually, a circle of light appears above you and begins to grow; you realize that you are actually moving upwards and that the circle of light is, paradoxically, sky. Inside a spacecraft? But there is no doubting it. You pass through the hole and find yourself in the middle of a rapidly flowing river under an alien sky. On either side are wide grass-covered plains. Soon you struggle over to the bank and leave the river, heading inland a short way. (From now on compass points will be used for directional references.) Turn to 102.

274

You start the revive cycle. After a few moments some sounds of activity arise from within the capsule, which then swings open, letting free a human being. Will you try to strike up a friendly conversation with this person (turn to **346**), or be a bit wary and threatening instead (turn to **310**)?

275

You spray the gas into the room. Roll one die and subtract the result from each of the STAMINAS of the guards:

First GUARD	STAMINA 4
Second GUARD	STAMINA 4

You use up the entire contents of the can – cross it off your Equipment List. If the guards are still alive, you will have to fight them (turn to **108**); otherwise turn to **203**.

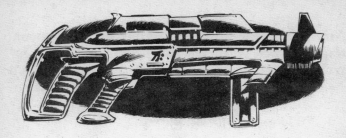

276

Roll one die. If the result is even, turn to **294**. If the result is odd, turn to **330**.

277

If you have just turned to this location, add 1 to your STATUS. Your vehicle is at point I, facing west. After checking your STATUS below, if you want to move ahead to point H, turn to **193**; if you want to turn on the spot to face north, turn to **241**. STATUS: if STATUS equals 7 or 8, turn to **123**; if it equals 1 or 16, turn to **66**; if it equals 15, turn to **188**. (Remember to return to **277**, though.)

278

You retreat in time to avoid the cables and showers of sparks. Obviously this hatch does not offer a way through, so you turn your attention to the other maintenance hatch. Turn to **77**.

279

As you have the steel-work of the gantry for cover, the machines will have some difficulty in hitting you.

	SKILL	STAMINA
First SENTINEL	4	9
Second SENTINEL	4	9

If you defeat them, turn to **351**.

280

'Wait! Wait!' Cyrus cries, flailing his arms in the air as you close in. 'Give a man about to lose his freedom one last request, a moment of reprieve!' You just look at him distrustfully. 'I'm a compulsive gambler,' he tells you. 'Will you play just one hand of cards with me?' Well, will you play (turn to **226**) or just grab him and finish it now (turn to **262**)?

281

As you race down the tunnel, tripping over the abundance of pipes, the voice continues:

DESTRUCTION IN T MINUS FIVE MINUTES

You come to another access hatch at the end of the tunnel, which you desperately fling open. On the other side is a room full of electronic circuitry rising from floor to ceiling. There is no obvious exit other than the hatch you have just opened. Will you explore the room in the hope of finding some hidden means of escape (turn to 317) or turn back and go down the other tunnel (turn to 353)?

282

As soon as you shoot, the aliens give a horrified scream and drop to the ground – into the cover of the thick grass. You approach the village giving the odd burst of fire into any likely looking clump of grass, sometimes eliciting a scream but generally hitting nothing. Without warning, most of the original aliens spring out of the grass only a matter of feet from you and cast short, needle-sharp spears with unerring accuracy. Most are turned by your armour but one or two find a chink to pierce, with fatal consequences. You stagger back a foot or so and collapse. You have failed.

283

The robot is a useless hulk, but directly underneath where it was standing you see a floor-safe, its button-covered dial previously hidden by the robot's feet. Looking closer you see there are three different coloured buttons to press to open it – blue, green and red. Intrigued, you decide to open it. Which colour button will you press first: blue (turn to 399), green (turn to 385) or red (turn to 376)?

284

'Ahem,' you say, clearing your throat, while nonchalantly leaning against a bulkhead. The man sits upright with a violent start and stares at you. He looks very upset. You explain to him your peaceful intentions and after a few minutes he loosens up and begins to talk freely, explaining that he is the technician responsible for maintaining the robots on board. His hatred for Cyrus is manifest. When you inquire as to why he dislikes Cyrus so much (especially as he works for him), he explains that they have been having 'problems' with the command robot on the bridge. Evidently this robot, a new experimental type, has developed a conscious personality and resents taking orders from Cyrus whom he (the robot) considers to be insane. Cyrus blames the technician for these problems and has ordered him to shut the command robot down, but the technician is especially unhappy about this, as he considers it would be murder. 'The machine is alive!' he explains. 'You only have to talk to him to see that. He knows he exists.' Finally, after this informative chat, the technician shows you how to open the security doors on the ship with an electronic key which he gives you. You leave through the other door. Turn to **356**.

285

If you chose the explosives, turn to **321**; if you chose the goggles, turn to **357**.

286

After a short distance you come to a fast-flowing river, which cuts across your path. Will you attempt to swim east, across the turgid waters (turn to **358**), or walk north (turn to **102**), west (turn to **214**) or south (turn to **122**)?

287

Rocks appear out of the water and cliffs rise on both sides as you hurtle south; ahead, the roar of white water increases. The boat is swept down through a series of water-slides, small waterfalls and jumbled rocks. Roll two dice. If the result *exceeds* your SKILL, you have lost control of your boat and fall out of it – roll one die and deduct the total from your STAMINA as you get dashed against some rocks. Eventually the rapids end and you are carried down the centre of a gigantic chasm. Turn to **324**.

288

You are on the edge of a vast impassable chasm which runs to the west and north, through the midst of the plains on which you stand (which continue to the south and east). In the bottom of the chasm you can see a wide lake teeming with life; there are also dark submerged shapes which might be large water animals or perhaps machines. There is no way to get down to find out. Will you follow the chasm north (turn to **160**) or west (turn to **227**), or leave the precipice and go south (turn to **253**) or east (turn to **104**)?

289

You climb into the midst of some low, rolling hills surrounded by a flat sea of grass. Will you explore these hills for a while (turn to **325**) or leave them (turn to **361**)?

290

Having vanquished the cleaners, you proceed down the corridor, but reach its end in very short time. The corridor terminates in the side of an enormous tunnel of at least twenty metres diameter, which disappears into darkness to the left and right. There are no lights in it and the only detail to be seen is a short landing which extends from the end of the corridor into the centre of the tunnel. The corridor has no doors leading from it other than one small maintenance hatch close to the tunnel end. Will you examine the hatch (turn to **125**) or the landing in the tunnel (turn to **362**)?

291

The man stirs as you approach and looks up with bleary eyes. He looks as if he has suffered terribly. 'Who are you?' he croaks through cracked lips. Will you tell him that you are an assassin sent to get Cyrus (turn to **363**) or that you are one of the crew of the *Vandervecken* (turn to **12**)?

292

Under your continually threatening gaze and provocative language the person suddenly metamorphoses into a hideous bat-like creature which swoops to attack you. Will you fight it (turn to **220**) or look in your pack for some other way out of the situation (turn to **256**)?

293

You sit back and take it easy for a bit – regain 5 points of STAMINA. After recuperating, you leave the kitchenette, and go into the security room and through the exit. Turn to **109**.

294

One of the octopus creatures catches the grenade in mid-flight with a couple of its tentacles and holds it aloft. The grenade explodes. Roll the usual dice to see how much damage each creature takes but, in addition, as the blast was so close to you, deduct 1 point from your own ARMOUR. Turn to **312**.

295

If you have any of the items below, choose which one you will employ and turn to the appropriate page:

Pan-Dimensional Homing Device	Turn to 377
Deck of playing cards	Turn to 367
Book of extra-terrestrials	Turn to 326
A Cephalo squirrel	Turn to 390

If you don't have any of these, you will either have to attempt to answer the creature's question (turn to 15) or fight it (turn to 383).

296

Opening your pack you clasp the matching part and raise it above your head, shouting: 'See, its brother returns!' The amazed aliens collapse to the ground and begin wailing. Raising one of the chiefs up, you convince him, via sign language, that he should give the part on the totem pole to you. When he understands, he signals to a younger alien who climbs the pole and returns with the part, which the chief then presents to you. Turn to 187.

297

You jump at a stout-looking pipe just above the opening and swing through the blazing crossfire out of the room. Safe! Turn to 369.

298

When you snap the goggles on, the room seems to light up. You can see Cyrus feeling his way along a wall (he is, unlike you, still blind in the darkness): he reaches a hanging picture and gives it a twist. To your surprise a small secret panel opens in the wall, through which Cyrus dives. The panel closes, becoming invisible. Well, you certainly have no reason to stay here, so you walk over to the picture, twist it, and dive through the secret panel when it opens. Turn to **171**.

299

Turn to **209**.

300

Stepping through the blast hole you find yourself in a small lock-up consisting of two cells and the room occupied by yourself and the now defunct guard. If you don't already have one, you may add the robot's assault blaster to your weaponry. The only exits from this lock-up are via an impassable security door and a small maintenance hatch which opens, you discover, into a narrow access tunnel leading into the dark interior of the spacecraft. Will you look in the first cell (turn to **63**), the second cell (turn to **318**) or leave the room via the tunnel (turn to **134**)?

301

You try to pass yourself off as a security guard. 'Just on a routine tour,' you say, 'checking IDs.' The machine muses for a bit before saying, 'I'll have to check with central. Just hold on . . .' It sits silent for a moment, evidently in contact with another section in the ship. Then, without warning, it attacks, and one of the shots slams into you – lose 1 ARMOUR point. You will have to fight it. Turn to **211**.

302

You carefully train your gun on the man – he remains still and silent. *Test your Luck*. If you are *Lucky*, turn to **212**. If you are *Unlucky*, turn to **338**.

303

The room, along with the Pillboxes, has been demolished. The only recognizable details left are the two exit doors – one is a standard security door while the other has two short black levers protruding from it. Both are a bit pockmarked, but still serviceable. Which will you take – the standard door (turn to **249**) or the door with levers (turn to **213**)?

304

You press the buttons on the homing device. Immediately, the beast decelerates to comic slow motion, the air glows orange and strange other-worldly scintillations arc about the cave. A door materializes in front of the monster which, as it steps across the threshold, vanishes from view – as if a curtain had been slowly drawn over it from head to tail. The door closes and evaporates. A hole appears in the ground, out of which a shortish green fellow climbs. 'One Scallopian Fang eradicated; that'll be either one weapon, *or* two grenades, *or* four pieces of armour, *or* any other piece of technology that you might have upon your person, such as a gravity bomb, infra-red goggles, nerve gas, etc. Failure to pay will result in your instantaneous transmission from this to another dimension.' If you cannot pay his price you have failed. If you can pay, delete the item(s) from your Equipment List and turn to **196**.

305

Roll three dice. If the result *exceeds* your STAMINA, turn to **45**. If the result is *equal to or less than* your STAMINA, you have made it safely across to the other bank – turn to **102**,

306

You are on the north side of a vast impassable chasm which runs from the west to east. The bottom is a flat plain. The plain you are standing on continues to the north, west and east; to the south you can see the other side of the chasm. Will you go north (turn to **84**) or west (turn to **179**), or follow the chasm east (turn to **252**)?

307

You avoid the shrubs. To the north, west and south you can see rolling grass-covered plains. To the east is a forest. Will you go north (turn to **179**), west (turn to **142**), south (turn to **26**) or east (turn to **343**)?

308

The corridor takes a sharp turn and thrusts you into a large room occupied by what appears to be a statue of an alien deity on a pedestal – strange deity, though, for it holds, in its six arms, six different weapons, some of them *very* modern. Its insectoid head contemplates you with uncountable eyes while its many limbs and sinuous body begin to writhe in a weird stop-go movement. Obviously it is *not* a statue! The thing leaps from its pedestal and attacks. During the battle it will use only one of its weapons per combat round; which weapon used is determined each combat round by rolling a die (see below). You may throw a grenade if you have one. Use the gunfire rules for all the deity's weapons.

	DIE ROLL	WEAPON	SKILL	STAMINA	DAMAGE
DEITY	1	whip	10		3
	2	bolos	9		2
	3	spear	7		1
	4	electric lash	8	12	2
	5	assault blaster	6		1–6
	6	disintegrator	5		instant destruction

If you defeat it, turn to **344**.

309

Behind the door is a path, floating in mid-air at a precipitous height over a wide and distant country-side. It must be miles below you, yet it is still within the *Vandervecken*. The path, looking tenuous and unreassuring, flies arrow-straight into the distance. You head across it, eventually arriving at a T-junction – the path splits and flies off in two new directions, neither offering a visible end to the possibility of a fatal drop. Will you follow the path left (turn to **345**) or right (turn to **50**)?

310

The occupant of the sleep capsule looks quite hurt, but, although he pouts a bit, he doesn't say anything. Will you stop threatening and try to be friendly (turn to **346**) or threaten the person some more (turn to **292**)?

311

You take out your deck of cards and ask the guards if they would like a game. Turn to **146**.

312

You fight them hand to hand. If you have read the book on mollusc nervous systems you inflict 1 extra point of damage every time you hit the creatures.

	SKILL	STAMINA
First MUTANT	8	8
Second MUTANT	8	6

If you defeat them, turn to **366**.

313

If you have just turned to this location, add 1 to your STATUS. Your vehicle is at point H, facing north. After checking your STATUS below, if you want to move ahead to point E, turn to **82**; if you want to turn on the spot to face west, turn to **193**; if you want to turn on the spot to face east, turn to **265**. STATUS: if STATUS equals 4 or 11, turn to **9**; if it equals 14, turn to **261**; if it equals 16, turn to **188**; if it equals 5, 6, 12 or 13, turn to **33**; if it equals 7, turn to **66**. (Remember to return to **313**, though.)

314

When you offer the can to the chief he takes it,
fiddles with it a bit, then presses the button on the
top – taking the spray directly in the face. He falls
over dead. The rest of the aliens are appalled and
leap at you with needle-sharp spears; the ferocity of
the attack breaches your armour. You collapse
under the wave of bodies, never to rise. You have
failed.

315

You jump, firing from the hip! Unfortunately, the
Sentinel below skids to one side, causing you to
land heavily on the floor. The ensuing crossfire from
the machines at point-blank range blows first your
armour and then you into atoms. You have failed.

316

Unfortunately, you succumb to the poison. You do not recover consciousness.

317

The voice booms out

T MINUS FOUR MINUTES

as you leap into the room and begin frantically searching. When the voice announces

T MINUS THREE MINUTES

you give up, jump back through the hatch and run down the other branch of the tunnel. Turn to **2**.

318

The second cell appears to be empty, but when you enter, a screaming little ball of fur and legs drops from above the door on to your shoulder. It is an Imp! You knock it off with a sharp clout, but not before it has damaged your armour with its fangs – lose 1 ARMOUR point. It scuttles back up the wall and glares down at you with red eyes. If you haven't already, you can look in the other cell (turn to 63); otherwise you leave the room via the maintenance hatch and tunnel (turn to 134).

319

The door slides to the side to expose a large laboratory. You don't have time to take in details, however, as a tiny silver sphere descends from a niche in the roof and hits you with a laser blast – lose 1 ARMOUR point. You will have to fight it.

LASER GLOBE   SKILL 9   STAMINA 1

If you defeat it, turn to 4.

320

'Freeze!' you yell, to attract his attention. He lowers his hands from his face and glares at you with red-rimmed eyes. You clamber into the room and demand of him that he tell you which way to go to reach Cyrus. He snorts derisively at you. 'Go through that door,' he indicates the security door, 'turn right and just follow the corridor.' You turn to the door, but he calls out, 'Here, you'll need this,' and throws you a small, narrow cylinder. 'It's a key for all the security doors.' You face the door, insert the key into a hole next to it and step through the doorway when it opens. Turn to 356.

321

The case contains two grenades. Add them to your weapon list, but do not count them towards pack limitations. Turn to **6**.

322

After a short distance you come upon a fast-flowing river which cuts across your path. Will you attempt to swim west, to the other side (turn to **7**) or walk either north (turn to **127**), east (turn to **83**) or south (turn to **160**)?

323

You are in a wide, open field surrounded by forest. Will you go north (turn to **121**), east (turn to **359**), west (turn to **27**) or south (turn to **115**)?

324

You are in the middle of a vast, still lake flanked by towering cliffs. Looking down into the water you notice a metallic glint from a large submerged shape. You dive down to investigate and are confronted by a small submarine, obviously in working order but currently unoccupied. A tug on your heel distracts you from your find, especially when you turn to see that a house-sized octopoid Bivalve has a firm grip on your leg with one of its tentacles. It drags you toward its shell. If you have read the book on mollusc nervous systems, turn to **47**; otherwise turn to **85**.

325

In a shallow dell you come across a small village of hemispherical adobe huts formed in a ring. In the centre of this ring you can see a totem pole. There is no movement or sign of life other than a few improbable-looking chickens scratching in the dust. If you haven't been here before, you may go down and have a closer look (turn to **246**); otherwise you decide to leave these hills (turn to **361**).

326

The book informs you that the creature is a Zark – a member of a race of extremely intelligent but friendless aliens whose greatest interest is, rather strangely, putting small furry creatures into boxes and trying to prove to them that *they* (the Zarks) are more intelligent and definitely more fun to be with than any small furry critter. If the critters beg to differ with the Zarks, then they quickly become just so much salad. Unfortunately, the book continues, the Zark, either through extreme boredom or short-sightedness, has chosen to demonstrate these facts to you. Will you attempt to answer the Zark's question (turn to **15**) or take this to be a rather pointless activity and fight it instead (turn to **383**)?

327

You leave the room, leap into the waiting commuter and zip back down the path, past the T-junction and along the left-hand branch. Turn to **70**.

328

You press the buttons on the homing device. Immediately, the monster slows to an improbable rate, the air glows orange and strange scintillations arc and criss-cross the room. A hole materializes under your foe and, as a consequence, it drops slowly out of sight. The hole then shrinks to a pinprick and evaporates. A small wooden hatch then slides out of the roof and, upon opening, extends an enormous green arm before your gaze. Its hand is open, as if asking for something. Looking closer you see this message tattooed on the palm: 'One Tharn Doppelgänger eradicated; that'll be either one weapon, or two grenades, or four pieces of armour, or any other piece of technology that you might have upon your person, such as a gravity bomb, infra-red goggles, nerve gas, etc. Failure to pay will result in your instantaneous transmission from this to another dimension.' If you cannot pay the price you have failed. If you can pay, delete the item(s) from your Equipment List and turn to **13**.

329
You approach the last pair; they are immobile and flank two identical doors. One of the devices rolls its eyes at you and says: 'The right door is the one *you* want.' 'Don't listen to him,' advises the other, 'he lies.' 'Only sometimes,' retorts the first. Which door will you go through – the right (turn to **131**) or the left (turn to **375**)?

330
The grenade lands in the pool and explodes, sending a huge spout of water to the roof and terrible shock-waves through the pool. Roll the dice for damage to the creatures and turn to **312**.

331
If you have just turned to this location, add 1 to your STATUS. Your vehicle is at point B, facing east. After checking your STATUS below, if you want to move ahead to point C, turn to **53**; if you want to turn on the spot to face south, turn to **91**. STATUS: if STATUS equals 3, turn to **33**; if it equals 4, 5, 11 or 12, turn to **66**; if it equals 10, turn to **188**. (Remember to return to **331**, though.)

332

The tunnel continues forward for a few hundred metres before ending at a landing. Alighting here, you find yourself at an opening into a room whose floor is covered by twenty very large and very odd tiles set out and decorated in the fashion illustrated on the opposite page (barring the numbers which, as you will see, are superimposed for reference only). You are standing on one side, while on the other side of the room there is a door which presents the only way forward. You know these tiles to be remarkable due to a small message which is engraved into the floor at your feet:

STEP ON THE WRONG TILE AND IT'S GOODBYE

Which tiles will you step on to reach the other side? When you have decided, add up all the numbers of the tiles you intend to step on and turn to the paragraph which equals that total. If the description on that page does not make sense (in context), then you have been blasted into your constituent atoms and will have to start the adventure again. Note: the numbers on the tiles have *nothing* to do with providing a solution to your problem.

333

You jump at a metal brace and swing for the opening but, horror of horrors, the brace snaps and sends you crashing to the floor between the two Sentinels. Their point-blank crossfire blasts you to atoms. You have failed.

334

You hear Cyrus scuffling around in the darkness. There is a click followed by silence. Meanwhile, you are searching for the light-switch. When you find it and turn it on, you see that Cyrus has disappeared. He couldn't have left through the door you entered by, as light would have come through the opening. There are no other exits – no visible exits anyway. You search for a secret door. *Test your Luck*. If you are *Lucky*, turn to **133**. If you are *Unlucky*, turn to **57**.

335

Will you go right (turn to **59**) or left (turn to **175**)?

336

The aliens halt their rush two metres or so from you, form into a wide column and begin a complicated shuffling dance, while another group of aliens, apparently singing, shuffle slowly out of the village. After the dance they lead you into the centre of the village, where a couple of obviously very important creatures officially welcome you in front of the totem pole. The pole is made of wood but is topped by something obviously not of their manufacture – a small black square indented with a large red button. If you would like to come into possession of this device, turn to **148**; otherwise turn to **350**.

337

As you depress the button, your world falls apart in soundless explosion – you never see what the safe had hidden. You have failed.

338

As you cock your gun, a loud *click* resounds from the weapon, alerting the man to your presence. His hands fly from his face and, seeing you, he dives from the bed into a corner, sending your first shot astray. He draws a pistol from under a rag in the corner. You shoot it out.

TECHNICIAN   SKILL 8   STAMINA 5

If you defeat him, turn to **248**.

339

'Nahh . . .' exclaims one. 'Don't lie to us,' says the other. Little panels flick open in their bodies, revealing multiple blasters. You will have to fight them. Turn to **71**.

340

The beast is almost upon you. Will you fight it (turn to **101**) or run away (turn to **139**)?

341

You are on a grass-covered plain which extends into the west, south and east. In the north you can see some low hills. A short distance away, in the centre of the plain, you can see what might be a wooden structure rising out of the grass. If you want to investigate it, turn to **215**; otherwise you can go north (turn to **289**), west (turn to **102**), south (turn to **83**) or east (turn to **159**).

342

You cross the room and open the box. Inside it are two large black levers side by side. Will you pull the left one (turn to **263**), the right one (turn to **299**) or leave the room alone (turn to **335**)?

343

You are surrounded by a forest of short white trees with blue foliage. Will you search the forest (turn to **217**), or go north (turn to **227**), west (turn to **235**), south (turn to **64**) or east (turn to **253**)?

344

The Deity collapses to the floor, smoke pouring at a furious rate from the dozen or so holes that you managed to smash into it. Through the thick atmosphere, on the other side of the room, you can see an exit. Will you inspect the remains of the Deity (turn to **218**) or leave via the other exit (turn to **254**)?

345

The path flies straight for a long while before ending in another T-junction. Looking down, you can still see the alien countryside, while to the left and right the path hangs in the air, precipitous and unending. Which way will you turn – left (turn to **70**) or right (turn to **219**)?

346

You start chatting quite pleasantly, although you don't learn anything new. The moment you become distracted, though, the person you are talking to metamorphoses into a hideous bat-like creature which attacks you. As you were taken completely by surprise the monster hits you, doing 1 point of damage to your ARMOUR. Turn to **220**.

347

You take out the container of ball-bearings and hold it above your head. 'Nobody move. This is a bomb that'll blow us all to atoms if you just so much as twitch.' You then cackle to add effect. Nobody likes a dangerous madman, least of all these domeheads. They stand very still. You make them lie down and throw away their blasters; while they are in this unprotected state, you easily gag and tie them up. The room has two other exits; one a security door and the other a simple sliding door. Which will you take: the security door (turn to **109**) or the sliding door (turn to **257**)?

348

You spray the mutants, but with little effect. In fact, the only thing you achieve is to empty the aerosol can – cross it off your Equipment List. You will have to fight the monsters. Turn to **204**.

349

If you have just turned to this location, add 1 to your STATUS. Your vehicle is at point A, facing south. After checking your STATUS below, if you want to move ahead to point D, turn to **130**; if you want to turn on the spot to face east, turn to **223**. STATUS: if STATUS equals 3 or 4, turn to **188**; if it equals 8 or 9, turn to **33**; if it equals 10, turn to **66**. (Remember to return to **349**, though.)

350

The creatures seem to be quite friendly, but to cement their goodwill you decide to give them a gift. What will you give them:

Aerosol can of nerve gas?	Turn to **314**
Enormous carnivore jaws?	Turn to **17**
A couple of pieces of orangey-purple fruit?	Turn to **35**
A piece of your technology?	Turn to **260**

If you don't have any of the first three, you will have to give the fourth.

351

The Sentinels are smoking piles of debris, littering the floor with smashed and burning parts. You stride past them and through the exit. Turn to **369**.

352

You struggle against unconsciousness and win! You stand up, reeling drunkenly. Through the miasma you see him standing by a table. You reach for your gun – you're going to get this fellow! Turn to **262**.

353

You scramble down into the unexplored passage. The voice booms:

T MINUS THREE MINUTES

You reach another maintenance hatch at the end of the tunnel. You fling it open. Turn to **40**.

354

Turn to **337**.

355

If you have just turned to this location, add 1 to your STATUS. Your vehicle is at point G, facing east. After checking your STATUS below, if you want to move ahead to point H, turn to **265**; if you want to turn on the spot to face north, turn to **73**. STATUS: if STATUS equals 1, turn to **28**; if it equals 7 or 16, turn to **33**; if it equals 8, turn to **66**. (Remember to return to **355**, though.)

356

The door opens on to a long, well-lit corridor stretching into the distance. Following it for a few minutes you come across a door set in the left-hand wall. Will you open this door (turn to **5**) or continue down the corridor (turn to **100**)?

357

The goggles are infra-red goggles. With them you will be able to see perfectly in the darkest of conditions. Turn to **6**.

358

Roll three dice. If the result *exceeds* your STAMINA, turn to **45**. If the result is *less than or equal to* your STAMINA, you have made it safely across to the eastern bank – turn to **250**.

359

You are in a forest of very tall bluish trees, all covered by extremely long thorns. There is some undergrowth in the form of shrubs and flowering bushes. As you pass by a particularly large shrub, it sends out a creeper which entwines itself around your legs. *Test your Luck*. If you are *Lucky*, turn to **8**. If you are *Unlucky*, you must fight the plant. If you do not kill the plant after three combat rounds it has dragged you into its mouth and killed you. The plant will not damage you unless it gets you into its mouth.

CARNIVOROUS
    PLANT   SKILL 0   STAMINA 6

If you defeat it, turn to **8**.

360

You climb into the tunnel and surface in a small room. It is quite obviously used to store garbage, which enters via a chute in the ceiling and, when there's enough of it, is tipped down the tunnel you just climbed up. There are two small maintenance hatches in the room; one is labelled ACCELERATOR 4B while the other has TRANSTUBE 113-24 stencilled on it. Both open into narrow access tunnels. Which will you enter: the accelerator tunnel (turn to **72**) or the transtube tunnel (turn to **129**)?

361

Will you go north (turn to **104**), west (turn to **253**), south (turn to **341**) or east (turn to **142**)?

362

The tunnel hangs around you like a dark, cavernous maw, as you walk out along the narrow landing. As soon as you reach the end, at the exact centre of the tunnel, you are swept off you feet by what feels like a powerful current of water. You fly down the centre of the tunnel, into the darkness, obviously being supported by an anti-gravity field. The sensation, after your initial alarm at being swept from your feet has worn off, is quite pleasant. You fly along in the dark for only a short period when another landing, leading to a door, appears in front of you. Will you attempt to leave the anti-gravity current at this landing (turn to **11**) or will you just drift for a while longer (turn to **49**)?

363

The man smiles, and tears of joy spring into his eyes: he tries to stroke your hand with a tentacle. The effort is a bit much though; his eyes start to roll and he looks as if he is about to lose consciousness. Before he does, he motions that he wants to whisper to you. 'Take the middle, always the middle.' He passes out. Turn to **327**.

364

You point the book which says: 'It's a Tharn Doppelgänger. Extremely dangerous but easy enough to get rid of – I'll just produce a random modulated tone . . .' A high-pitched whistle then emanates from the book but, instead of scaring the monster away, it seems to infuriate it even more. You fight it hand to hand.

THARN
DOPPELGÄNGER   SKILL 9   STAMINA 6

If you defeat it, turn to **13**.

365

If you have just turned to this location, add 1 to your STATUS. Your vehicle is at point C, facing west. After checking your STATUS below, if you want to move ahead to point B, turn to **167**; if you want to turn on the spot to face south, turn to **53**. STATUS: if STATUS equals 4, 5 or 12, turn to **176**; if it equals 3, turn to **66**; if it equals 10 or 11, turn to **33**; if it equals 1 or 2, turn to **188**. (Remember to return to **365**, though.)

366

The bodies of the creatures float gently on the surface of the pool. You run to the exit. Turn to **373**.

367

You shuffle the cards and try to think of some trick to confound the creature. 'If I have fifty-two cards of normal design here,' you begin, 'and I take out two, one of which you know to be of greater value than seven . . .' 'Ace high?' it asks, suspicious. 'Of course,' you continue; 'I then remove at least five other cards, of which two are specified by you, two by me and one or more left up to chance. Furthermore, if I now take out the highest card left in the pack and place it to one side – what is the probability of successfully guessing the value of the card that is twelfth in value behind the second highest card in the deck?' *Test your Luck*. If you are *Lucky*, turn to **149**. If you are *Unlucky*, turn to **259**.

368

The creatures form a crush around you and lead off to the south, singing and dancing all the while. After a number of kilometres you leave the hills and cross a grass-covered plain, arriving, eventually, at a pier in a river. The aliens make it obvious that they want you to have one of the sturdy-looking canoes tethered there. Will you take one of the canoes and paddle downstream (turn to **96**) or will you decline their offer and leave the tribe by foot (turn to **168**)?

The opening leads into a narrow corridor which, after twisting and winding for a while, ends in a door. Going through this you find yourself in what is obviously the ship's bridge; there are panoramic visuals, holographic plotters and maps, and scores of comlinks. In front of you, standing before a control panel with which it is connected by an umbilical cord, is the ship's pilot – a stunningly wrought humanoid robot. Its chromium limbs send reflections skittering across the walls as it turns to face you. 'Ah, you've arrived,' it says, almost smiling. 'I've been quite looking forward to chatting with such an interesting person.' Will you talk with the pilot (turn to **18**) or assume it's trying to get your guard down and attack it (turn to **94**)?

370

As you dive at him again he throws the device in your face while scuttling nimbly to the other side of the room, where he gives a hanging picture a sharp twist. A small secret panel opens and Cyrus dives through. The panel shuts. You notice that the device that Cyrus threatened you with is nothing more than the clockwork mechanism from an ancient clock. 'Must be his hobby,' you mutter to yourself as you twist the picture to open the secret panel. When it obliges, you dive through into a chute, after the scientist. Turn to **171**.

371

Turn to 288.

372

The crate is almost full of an orangey-purple fruit. As you stir it around a bit with one hand, you notice that all the squirrel-things have become silent and are staring hungrily at you. Will you taste a bit of the fruit (turn to 388), pocket a few pieces (turn to 393) or leave everything in the room alone and proceed along the corridor outside (turn to 118)?

373

Through the opening is a chamber occupied by a brutish-looking extra-terrestrial draped in large sheets of armour-plate and toting a whopping great disintegrator – aimed at you. In the wall behind this unfriendly being are three large circular doors. 'Stop!' it says, peering at you with a pair of close-set beady eyes. 'To pass, you must answer my question . . . if you think you are intelligent enough.' Will you attempt to answer the creature's as yet unasked question (turn to **15**), look in your pack for some other means of passing it (turn to **295**), or forget about niceties and just blast it (turn to **383**)?

374

If you have just turned to this location, add 1 to your STATUS. Your vehicle is at point D, facing north. After checking your STATUS below, if you want to move ahead to point A, turn to **223**; if you want to turn on the spot to face east, turn to **380**. STATUS: if STATUS equals 8, turn to **188**; if it equals 10, turn to **261**; if it equals 9, turn to **66**. (Remember to return to **374**, though.)

375

You open the door and are engulfed by a fierce, blue, electric fire. Roll three dice and subtract the total from your STAMINA. If this hasn't killed you, then you slam this door shut and go through the other – turn to **131**.

376

The button depresses, making the safe's dial pulsate with a fluorescent white light. Which button will you press next – blue (turn to 354) or green (turn to 205)?

377

You press the two buttons on the device. An orange light pervades the room as white vapours arc around the creature. A small cage-like elevator materializes around the frozen alien which is then winched away by unseen forces through the ceiling of the room. The weird light subsides a bit before this message floats in front of you: 'One Zark eliminated; payment for this service will be either one weapon, *or* two grenades, *or* four pieces of armour, *or* any other piece of technology that you might have upon your person, such as a gravity bomb, infra-red goggles, nerve gas, etc. Failure to pay will result in your instantaneous transmission to the dimension of our choice.' If you cannot pay the price, then you have failed, otherwise cross the item(s) from your Equipment List and turn to 97.

378

Brushing past the sign and strolling down a short corridor, you enter a room whose surfaces all glow with a faint greenish light. Odd. There are large cracks in all the walls, through which thousands of shiny granules or pellets have poured, spilling across the floor. You pick a handful of these up to have a closer look. You recognize them as being plutonium pellets, which means that you have certainly received a fatal dose of radiation – enough to kill you within hours and immobilize you within minutes. You slump to the floor in despair, awaiting your doom. You have failed.

379
You manage to back one of the squirrel-things into a corner, then, with a leap, you snare it. It squeals a bit but does not try to escape from your grasp; instead, it looks at you with wide imploring eyes and stretches a couple of paws toward the open crate. Stepping over to this, you see that it is almost full of an orangey-purple fruit. When the critter sees the fruit it stretches even harder, as if to grasp a tasty morsel. Will you give the little fellow a piece of the fruit (turn to **186**), try a piece yourself first (turn to **388**), or just ignore the crate and, with the squirrel-thing, leave the room and proceed along the corridor (turn to **118**)?

380
If you have just turned to this location, add 1 to your STATUS. Your vehicle is at point D, facing east. After checking your STATUS below, if you want to move ahead to point E, turn to **386**; if you want to turn on the spot to face north, turn to **374**; if you want to turn on the spot to face south, turn to **130**. STATUS: if STATUS equals 8, turn to **188**; if it equals 6, turn to **261**; if it equals 14 or 15, turn to **123**; if it equals 13, turn to **161**; if it equals 2, turn to **28**; if it equals 9, turn to **66**. (Remember to return to **380**, though.)

You go through the door and into a dark, cluttered room; all sorts of monitoring equipment, crash couches, controls and visuals are crammed into the tiny amount of available space. Seating yourself in the most comfortable-looking of the eight or nine chairs present, you cast about for some purpose to all this. Suddenly, the lights fail, your chair sinks into the floor and a synthesized voice starts up: 'Congratulations, you have selected the ''Let's fight to the finish'' scenario of the street-fighting war-game. You will be commanding an XM3 Main Battle Assault Vehicle armed with a 4000 Bevawatt Phaser while your opponent will be using the lighter but faster US11 Tank Destroyer armed with a 6000 Bevawatt Phaser. Good luck.' The lights come back on. You are at the controls of an armoured assault vehicle. Through the single visual scanner in the cockpit (which, dangerously, only allows you to see what is to the front of your vehicle and nothing to the side or rear), you can see a couple of blocks of flats.

You will now have to learn a few rules of combat. Turn to the back of the book and you will see a map of the area in which you will be fighting and a score-sheet for use with this scenario.

The Vehicles: Instead of using your own ARMOUR or STAMINA in this battle, you will be using the SHIELDS of the vehicles. Your vehicle's defence level is 5 SHIELDS while your opponent's is only 4. Note the section set aside on the score-sheet for scoring hits against each other – the numbers are there to cross off as hits are given or received. Each hit received will reduce the number of SHIELDS carried by 1. When the number of SHIELDS carried by a vehicle reaches zero then that vehicle and its occupant are destroyed. When you fire at your opponent, roll two dice. If the result is *less than* your SKILL, you have hit your opponent. If the result is *equal to or greater than* your SKILL, then you have missed. Enemy fire – when it occurs – will be explained during the battle.

Status: STATUS is used to move your opponent's vehicle around the battlefield. During the course of the battle you will be instructed to change your STATUS and to check it against certain values provided – it is essential that you follow *all* instructions regarding it. Its value progresses from 1 to 16; if your STATUS reaches 17, then reduce it to 1. Every time you move your vehicle to a new location *or* turn on the same spot, you must add 1 to your STATUS (there are continual reminders at each location to do this, so you shouldn't forget). If you use the score-sheet, you should easily be able to keep track of your STATUS. Your STATUS now, just before starting, is zero – circle this value now, and all future additions for easy reference. This should all become a lot clearer once you begin.

Moving: It is absolutely essential to use the map to keep track of your location on the battlefield, as reference to movement is given in terms of the points on the map (A, B, C, D, E, F, G, H, I). Your vehicle must continually move – you cannot sit in one location and wait for your opponent to appear. Turn to **223**.

382

The spheres part before you as you stride boldly forward. Over the other side and through the door you find yourself in a high-ceilinged hall. Down both sides of this hall, standing on short stone pedestals, is a small but weird collection of simulated life-forms. They stand, facing one another across the floor – aluminium birds, tungsten-steel turtles with six legs, and creatures you don't even recognize. There are eight in all. You walk slowly down the middle of the room. As you draw level with the first pair they come to life, swivelling slightly to face you.

'The moon is red, the sky is pink,' says the first. 'Which is faster, light or time?' asks the second. What will you answer – light (turn to **89**) or time (turn to **225**)?

383

Note that the extra-terrestrial is armed with a disintegrator which will destroy you instantly with just one hit.

ZARK   SKILL 5   STAMINA 7

If you defeat it, turn to **392**.

384

Still firing at the monster, you run out of time, drifting straight into its cavernous maw. With one bite of its many teeth it finishes you. You have failed.

385

Turn to **337**.

386

If you have just turned to this location, add 1 to your STATUS. Your vehicle is at point E, facing east. After checking your STATUS below, if you want to move ahead to point F, you can either turn to **110** (to finish facing north) or to **136** (to finish facing south); if you want to turn on the spot (E) then turn to **82** to face north, or to **22** to face south. STATUS: if STATUS equals 6, 13 or 14, turn to **66**; if it equals 5 or 12, turn to **188**; if it equals 2, turn to **176**; if it equals 15, turn to **261**. (Remember to return to **386**, though.)

387

'Right,' says one. 'Yup,' says the other. The turn away and stare at the ceiling. Walking past these, you are hailed by the next couple. 'Hey, you, helmet-head . . .' cries the first. 'Yeah, where are you going?' asks the other. What will you answer: the truth, that you are trying to find Cyrus (turn to 221), or a fabrication, that you are inspecting the ship as part of a security check (turn to 339)?

388

Lifting the visor on your helmet, you take one bite of the fruit and then black out, never recovering consciousness. You have failed.

389

'Yeah, yeah,' you say, waving aside the robot's question. 'Look, all that garbage aside, I want to know where . . .' 'Yes,' cuts in the pilot, icily, 'I know what you want, *pleb*. I know what you *think* you want, and I know where you can find him. But, I also know what you actually want, what you really need.' 'What?' you ask, wondering what super-weapon the pilot is going to reveal for your use. 'What you really need is . . . *this!*' The robot presses a switch on the control panel. Instantly, panels in the floor and ceiling slide away, allowing the stasis generators hidden behind them to grip you in a glove of timelessness. Frozen, unconscious and in enemy hands, you have failed.

390

The squirrel-thing jumps from your grasp and bounds over toward the extra-terrestrial. If you fed the squirrel-thing some of the orangey-purple fruit earlier, turn to **111**; otherwise turn to **92**.

391

If you have just turned to this location, add 1 to your STATUS. Your vehicle is at point F, facing west. After checking your STATUS below, if you want to move ahead to point E, turn to **216**; if you want to turn on the spot to face north, turn to **110**; if you want to turn on the spot to face south, turn to **136**. STATUS: if STATUS equals 6, turn to **176**; if it equals 9, turn to **123**; if it equals 13, turn to **9**; if it equals 1, turn to **188**; if it equals 2 or 15, turn to **66**; if it equals 14, turn to **33**. (Remember to return to **391**, though.)

392

The Zark is destroyed but, to your disappointment, no doubt, you find that its disintegrator is designed in such an unearthly fashion that you cannot use it. You inspect the three doors in the opposite wall. Turn to **97**.

393

You slip a few pieces of the fruit in your pack, then, seeing nothing else of interest, you leave the room and continue along the corridor. Turn to **118**.

394

You rip the sachet open and sprinkle the contents liberally over both mutants. Eyes glaze over, tentacles ripple back into tiny knotted balls and the clicking increases to a high-pitched squeal. They both drop into the water and disappear into dense clouds of smoky-black ink. You run the rest of the distance to the exit. Turn to **373**.

weightless. He scrambled to his feet, two
thousand feet in the air. A sudden surge of
nausea made him retch, he felt a thin stream
of something that was cold. Fullness in his mouth

395

Behind the door is a biological laboratory and, evidently, museum. There are whole shelves full of grisly reminders of some of Cyrus's previous experiments on living creatures: whole organs and limbs are preserved in jars in long rows reaching to the ceiling. Not all the remains are human. On an operating table in the centre of the room, surrounded by instruments of surgery, is the prone and unconscious figure of a man with tentacles instead of arms. He is strapped down. Will you go up to the man (turn to 291) or give the whole nasty scene a wide berth (turn to 327)?

396

You press the buttons on the homing device. Immediately, the guards are surrounded by a pulsing orange light which seems to freeze them. After a moment, a pair of revolving doors materialize around them and promptly turn, taking the unwitting security officers out of sight. The doors continue to turn around a couple of times before evaporating. There is no sign of the guards. The floor of the room (apart from the few tiles you are standing on) disappears as well, to reveal a truly enormous giant standing on some hyperspatial mountain. It speaks: 'Payment for those two will be either two weapons, *or* four grenades, *or* eight pieces of armour, *or* any two other pieces of technology that you might possess, such as a gravity bomb, infra-red goggles, nerve gas, etc. Failure to pay will result in your instantaneous transmission from this dimension to another, of my choice.' If you cannot pay this price, then you have failed. If you can pay, delete the items from your Equipment List and turn to **203**.

397

Will you go north (turn to **142**), west (turn to **341**), south (turn to **121**) or east (turn to **26**)?

398

The corridor continues for a very long while and still stretches into the distance when you come across another security door on the side. This one is stencilled:

CEPHALO SQUIRRELS
HANDLE WITH CARE

Will you enter this room (turn to **230**) or continue down the corridor (turn to **118**)?

399

Turn to 337.

400

You drag the unconscious Cyrus from the Waldo. Your mission is a complete success. Congratulations.

GAME GRID

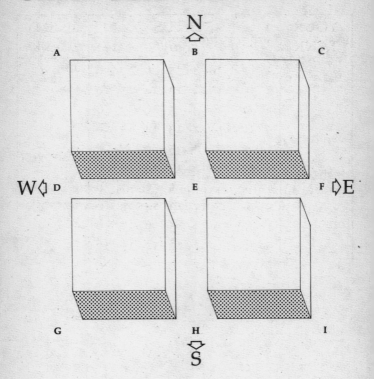

SCORE SHEET

YOUR TANK	STATUS							ENEMY TANK
	zero							
5	1	2	3	4	5	6	7	8	4
4	9	10	11	12	13	14	15	16	3
3	1	2	3	4	5	6	7	8	2
2	9	10	11	12	13	14	15	16	1
1	1	2	3	4	5	6	7	8	destroyed
destroyed	9	10	11	12	13	14	15	16	
	1	2	3	4	5	6	7	8	
	9	10	11	12	13	14	15	16	
	1	2	3	4	5	6	7	8	
	9	10	11	12	13	14	15	16	

Steve Jackson's

SORCERY! 1

THE SHAMUTANTI HILLS

Your search for the legendary Crown of Kings takes you to the Shamutanti Hills. Alive with evil creatures, lawless wanderers and bloodthirsty monsters, the land is riddled with tricks and traps waiting for the unwary traveller. Will you be able to cross the hills safely and proceed to the second part of the adventure – or will you perish in the attempt?

SORCERY! 2

KHARÉ – CITYPORT OF TRAPS

As a warrior relying on force of arms, or a wizard trained in magic, you must brave the terror of a city built to trap the unwary. You will need all your wits about you to survive the unimaginable horrors ahead and to make sense of the clues which may lead to your success – or to your doom!

SORCERY! 3

THE SEVEN SERPENTS

Seven deadly and magical serpents speed ahead of you to warn the evil Archmage of your coming. Will you be able to catch them before they get there?

SORCERY! 4

THE CROWN OF KINGS

At the end of your long trek, you face the unknown terrors of the Mampang Fortress. Hidden inside the keep is the Crown of Kings – the ultimate goal of the *Sorcery!* epic. But beware! For if you have not defeated the Seven Serpents, your arrival has been anticipated . . .

Complete with all the magical spells you will need, each book can be played either on its own, or as part of the whole epic.

FIGHTING FANTASY

The introductory Role-playing game

Steve Jackson

The world of Fighting Fantasy, peopled by Orcs, dragons, zombies and vampires, has captured the imagination of millions of readers world-wide. Thrilling adventures of sword and sorcery come to life in the Fighting Fantasy Gamebooks, where the reader is the hero, dicing with death and demons in search of villains, treasure or freedom.

Now YOU can create your own Fighting Fantasy adventures and send your friends off on dangerous missions! In this clearly written handbook, there are hints on devising combats, monsters to use, tricks and tactics, as well as two mini-adventures complete with GamesMaster's notes for you to start with. Literally countless adventures await you!

WHAT IS DUNGEONS AND DRAGONS?

John Butterfield, Philip Parker, David Honigmann

A fascinating guide to the greatest of all role-playing games: it includes detailed background notes, hints on play and dungeon design, strategy and tactics, and will prove invaluable for players and beginners alike.

Another Adventure Gamebook

MAELSTROM

Alexander Scott

Imagine a band of travellers on the long road from St Albans to London – a dangerous journey in troubled times. Which will YOU be – an alchemist, skilled in the dark arts of magick, a rogue on the run from justice, a noble lady on her way to stir up intrigue at court, a spy disguised as a herbalist carrying vital messages to the King, or any one of a host of different characters . . .

YOU choose the characters, YOU decide the missions and YOU have the adventures in the turbulent world of Europe in the sixteenth century – either as a player or as the referee.

Complete with Beginners' and Advanced Rules, Referee's Notes, maps, charts and a solo adventure to get you started, *Maelstrom* is a great game for three or more players.